HDO

SURVIVAL!

CAVE-IN

ST. CLAIRE, PENNSYLVANIA, 1859

K. DUEY AND K. A. BALE

ALADDIN PAPERBACKS

FOR THE WOMEN WHO TAUGHT US THE MEANING OF COURAGE:

ERMA L. KOSANOVICH
KATHERINE B. BALE
MARY E. PEERY

———————————

First Aladdin Paperbacks edition November 1998

Copyright © 1998 by Kathleen Duey and Karen A. Bale

Aladdin Paperbacks
An imprint of Simon & Schuster
Children's Publishing Division
1230 Avenue of the Americas
New York, NY 10020

Library of Congress Cataloging-in-Publication Data
Duey, Kathleen.
Cave-in, St. Claire, Pennsylvania, 1859 / by K. Duey and K.A. Bale.
— 1st Aladdin Paperbacks ed.
    p.   cm. — (Survival! ; #7)
Summary: In 1859 when Rory disguises herself as a boy in order to work in a
coal mine in St. Claire, Pennsylvania, she and her friend struggle to survive a
cave-in disaster.
ISBN 0-689-82350-9 (pbk.)
[1. Coal mines and mining—Fiction. 2. Survival—Fiction.]
I. Bale, Karen A. II. Title. III. Series: Duey, Kathleen. Survival! bk. 7
          PZ7.D8694Cav   1998
          [Fic]—dc21   98-42122
                CIP   AC

CHAPTER ONE

Liam Quinn shouted for the trapper boy to open the last door. Passing through it, he smiled his thanks, then went on. The gangway was crowded. Miners' lamps bobbed in the darkness. He walked the narrow path between the backed-up coal cars and the rib, one shoulder sliding along the rough rock wall.

Liam nodded at the mule drivers as he passed them. Some were impatient, swearing and spitting. The mules were happy enough to rest; most were standing with one hip up, their heads low. As he got closer to the clamor of the shaft engines and the furnace, Liam saw what was causing the delay. Loads of oats and hay were being brought down, and the mule drivers were waiting for the shaft's elevator cages to clear.

The furnace was roaring today, Liam noticed. The miners had been complaining about the bad air here in the Mammoth Vein. Maybe the bosses had listened for once. Da said firing up the furnace wasn't enough. He thought there should be more doors to force the air out into the rooms where the miners worked.

Liam had overheard a hundred arguments on the topic. But conditions were better than they had been two years before when the big firedamp explosion had burned the breaker to the ground. Kirk and Baum had been pouring money into the colliery since they'd bought it. Maybe, with better ventilation, there'd never be another buildup of the explosive gas.

Liam worked his way toward the knot of men around the cages. They were unloading mule feed onto empty coal cars to be hauled away. The mules plodded along the curved siding that ran down the stable gangway. They placed their hooves between the ties, judging each step perfectly, automatically. Most of them hadn't seen the sun or walked anywhere but between iron rails for years.

"That's it!" someone shouted.

Liam heard the cracking of a driver's whip and watched the first mule in line pull its heavy load of coal into the open cage, walking straight through to be unhitched on the far side. The coal car was left standing on the section of track built into the cage floor. Another shout and the operator pulled back the lever. The cage swung a little under the tonnage as the car rose upward.

Liam walked between the engines and started up the ladder. He wondered what the day was like—Rory had told him the whole week had been sunny. Above his head was a patch of dim grayish light; the shaft opening was inside the breaker building.

Halfway up, Liam paused, hooking one arm through the ladder rungs. He didn't look down. On either side of him the pumps were working; he could feel the vibration in the rock. The number two cage came past, going up, and Liam looked inside.

The mine car was loaded high with glittery black coal. It looked wet. Liam had heard that none of the low lifts in the Seven-Foot Vein was flooded except the sump close to the new slope. Here in the Mammoth, they had one big wet section—but even with the pumps acting up, it was still dry where he and Da were. The miner's tag tied to the back of the car fluttered, and Liam tried to read the name and number, but couldn't.

Liam patted his overalls pocket, assuring himself that his cap and light were safe. Then he started up the ladder again, going as quickly as he could. He wouldn't get a bite of dinner until he got back down to where his father was still working, undercutting the second face of the day.

As Liam topped the ladder, he stood for a second, watching the number two cage ascend. It swung slightly from its chains as it was hauled upward. The top of the breaker was five stories overhead, and Liam waited until the operator up there had locked the cage into place before he went on.

Liam started up the steps. The planks were coated with a fine black grit that stuck to the soles of his rubber boots. The huge crusher and the cylinder with its iron-bar separating screens had been turning without pause for weeks in spite of the trouble with the pumps. Liam prayed every night that the water level wouldn't work mischief on so many gangways that they lost the air. The St. Claire colliery had been closed more than once because of bad ventilation. Without clean air flowing through to sweep out the mine gas, firedamp had formed. A bad firedamp explosion in '56 had shut down the whole works for several months.

Liam cringed at the metallic din around him. High overhead he heard the deafening clatter as the car was tipped, its four tons of coal sliding out onto the shaker. As the coal started down the long row of chutes, the noise blended into the constant, creaking roar of the turning shafts and revolving cylinder.

At the top of the first flight of steps, Liam glanced back toward the shaft. The cage was going back down, the coal car empty now. Number one was rising again. Liam watched it for a second, wishing his brother Padraic could join Da and him underground. Nowhere was worse than up here in the breaker.

The air was thick with coal dust. Liam went up one more flight, then turned and walked out onto a platform above the long chutes. It took him a minute to spot Paddy, hunched over his chute, his cap and jacket black with the dust. Liam knew full well the ache from the hard wood benches and the seeping cold that came from sitting still, hour after hour, bent over the sliding coal that came down endlessly from the top of the breaker.

There were two old men on this shift, Liam saw. One had a crutch propped against his chute. He was missing one leg. Liam knew him. He had been caught in a cave-in years before. His leg had been crushed, and he was lucky to be alive, but he couldn't work underground anymore. Breaker boys often became miners. Miners sometimes turned back into breaker boys.

Another car full of coal dumped into the chutes high overhead. There was an ear-splitting clamor, then the rending grind of the crusher.

Liam counted to three and heard the numbing rattle begin again as the coal entered the cylinder that screened it, separating it into different sizes.

The breaker boss stood behind the benches, straddling two chutes on the slanted floor, standing on boards identical to the ones the boys sat upon. He looked bored, almost sleepy, but he held a sawed-off broom handle, and his eyes, Liam was sure, were roving back and forth over the hunched figures in front of him.

Liam squinted. Paddy had steamboat coal today, so the chunks were big. They looked dirty. Liam could see pieces of gray slate. Even the cleaners at the lowest benches were working hard, bent low, their hands flying.

Liam watched the cleaner on the chestnut chute. He tossed the little nut-sized shards of slate into the waste chute without looking. Only once that he was sure every bit of rock was removed did he lift his feet and let the coal slide downward toward the huge hoppers above the railroad track.

Liam had never been a cleaner and had never

wanted to be. He could make a nickel more a day, but the boss would always be looking over his shoulder. Any cleaner who let much slate get past him would soon be trading benches with someone else.

Liam turned to his brother. The boy next to Paddy was quite a bit older, but his fingers looked painfully swollen and they were as pink as a rich girl's hair ribbon. He was new, Liam was sure, and he had a bad case of red tips. Without meaning to, Liam closed his own hands into fists, remembering. The sulfur in the coal muck was what did it, Da had told him.

Paddy's hands had hardened against the sulfur, but they were chapped and cracked deep enough to bleed some nights. The breaker boss forbade any of the boys to wear gloves, no matter how cold it got—gloves made them slow and clumsy.

As Liam watched, two of the boys began to talk, leaning close enough to shout into each other's ear over the din of the grinding machinery. Liam glanced at the breaker boss, standing behind the rows of benches. The boys kept talking. The breaker boss moved toward them, walking the edges of the chutes, placing his feet carefully. When he was behind them, he waited a few more seconds, slapping the broom handle into his palm.

Liam winced as the boss struck one boy, then the other. The smaller one was knocked off balance and lurched forward, falling face first into the coal. The boss picked him up by his collar and set him back on his bench just as the dinner signal blew.

The steam whistle penetrated even the squealing roar of the breaker's machinery, and every boy looked up instantly. The breaker boss shouted, and they faced their work again, sorting coal from rock until they lifted their feet, letting the last of the coal slide past them. Only then did they stand and bolt for the steps. The breaker boss shouted again, but his shout was lost in the last rending groan of the cylinder overhead and the final grating slide of coal into the hoppers below.

The breaker boys grabbed their dinner pails from the stack near the door. Liam pattered down the steps, crossing the metal chutes, sure-footed in his rubber boots.

"Paddy!" Liam shouted, but his brother didn't slow down. Liam knew from experience that Paddy's hearing would be dull for most of the dinner hour, and that it would take more than a shout to get his attention. Pushing his way through the boys who crowded around their dinner pails, ignoring the scowl on the breaker boss's face, Liam came up behind his brother and laid a hand on his shoulder.

Startled, Paddy whipped around, his pale face shadowed with coal dust and tight with wariness. When he saw Liam, he grinned. "What are you doing up here?"

Liam tugged at Paddy's cap. "Da sent me to see if you were making out all right today."

Paddy nodded, stepping back. "Fine. I'm fine."

As he started down the steps, Liam fell in beside him. "Are you warm enough? Da said I was to go home and get you the extra shirt if you weren't."

Paddy glanced up at him as they rounded the

last landing and went downward again. Ahead of them, Liam heard boys whooping as they hit the ground, running for their favorite spot along the sunny side of the breaker building.

"I'll be all right," Paddy said as they emerged into the autumn sunlight.

Liam blinked, his eyes watering in the glaring brightness of the full midday sun. He wiped at them. Coal dust hung in the air along with the sharp smell of molten iron that came out of the foundry next door.

"You eat yet?" Paddy asked.

Liam shook his head. "Da made me come up here first."

"Then you don't have to stay, Liam," Paddy told him. "Just tell Da I'm fine."

Liam began to nod just as Paddy cleared his throat, then coughed. The cough bent him double. Liam could hear the deep wheezing in his chest. When the spasm finally subsided, he waved one hand at Liam. "You tell Da I'm fine. I can't stop working or they'll replace me in a day and you know it."

Liam glanced across the barren clearing

around the breaker building to the mountain of culm on the far side. Some of the boys were over there already, their food eaten. Liam saw one boy pick up a piece of shale and throw it at another. Instantly, a full-scale rock-war was in progress. The boys' shouts and laughter echoed against the brick chimney of the foundry.

Liam forced himself to turn back to Paddy, wishing his face was rosy instead of ashen, that he was strong and healthy and laughing like the other boys. But he never had been. Instead, he was pale, stubborn, hardworking, and good-hearted. Liam reached out to tousle Paddy's hair, but he ducked away. The laughter brought on another coughing fit that lasted until they were beside the other groups of boys who sat in the sunshine, talking and eating.

"Quinn!" one of them shouted. "Paddy Quinn, come join us. Ryan's got a newspaper story to read."

"You go eat your dinner, Liam," Paddy said.

Liam watched him go. Paddy was ten—two years younger than he should have been to work in the breaker. And he was small for his years as well. Most of the boys were taller and heavier, but Liam saw them turning, each greeting Paddy with a grin or a friendly slap on the shoulder as he passed. No one was likely to play too rough a trick on Paddy. It had been like that all his life; Paddy's smile could charm a snake.

Liam started back to the shaft, wondering if he would have time to eat dinner before Da needed him to start loading again. Mrs. Hamilton and Rory had been at the stove all week long, and his tin had stew and a slice of pie as well as the regular mutton and potatoes. His mouth watered, thinking about it. They were lucky, and he knew it. A lot of boarding-house widows were far less accommodating than Mrs. Hamilton.

At the shaft, the big cable wheels turning overhead, Liam headed for the ladder, but at that instant an empty coal car was coming downward, and he paused without thinking. The operator slowed the cage, making sure it went into the shaft straight and square. Liam sprinted toward it. Ignoring the operator's shout, he jumped in as it lowered, then stood, bracing himself against the side of the empty coal car.

The masonry that lined the upper part of the shaft slid past, and Liam laughed aloud, knowing Da would be angry if anyone told him, but still glad he had jumped the cage. The masonry changed to planking as the cage went downward and the light of day dimmed into a tiny square above his head.

The near silence of the mine was welcome as the cage bumped down, settling against the bottom of the shaft. The rails lined up perfectly, and Liam excused himself, stepping around the mule driver who was waiting to rehitch to the empty car.

Liam pulled his cap and light from his pocket. He settled the cap onto his head, shoving it down around his ears. Then he pushed his light into place, making sure the strap was tight enough to support the weight of the little silver can that held his supply of coal oil. Fishing matches from his pocket, he lit the wick by feel alone and was rewarded with a pale circle of light.

As the mule and car went past, Liam pushed his matchbox deep into his pocket. He glanced back toward the shaft, just to see the diffused sunlight that filtered through the breaker windows. Then he started walking.

Liam's stomach was rumbling with hunger as he followed the iron rails down the gangway. He hurried, walking into the ink-black darkness of the mine. Ahead he could see a bobbing miner's lamp, but the man, whoever he was, turned off the main tunnel, and the light winked out of sight.

Liam slowed only when the ceiling lowered and he had to duck his head. The muted sound of mule's hooves on the ties behind him made him step aside, pressing his back against the rough stone wall.

"Quinn? What are you doing up here this time of day?"

Liam recognized the driver and grinned. "Hey, Nolan! Had to go see my brother."

"How's he doing?" Nolan jumped down off the bumper of the coal car, calling out to his mule to stop. He threw one arm over the animal's neck, leaning companionably against her, scratching her ears.

"Paddy's all right," Liam said. He liked Nolan and he liked his mule, a good-natured jenny named Lucky. She had spent most of her life underground—her long ears had been worn down from the constant rub of the low ceilings.

"In a year or so he can come down with you and your Da," Nolan said. "Then it'll all be better."

"I hope it's long before that," Liam answered. "Can you get a little time to go fishing next Sunday?"

Nolan nodded. "Best thing about having no church here. No mass, and more time to fish."

Liam laughed with him and stood clear as Nolan climbed onto his perch on the coal car. Nolan spoke, and Lucky started forward, digging in her blunt hooves, straining to get the car rolling again. A blur of motion caught Liam's eye. Rats. That was good. Usually the air in this part of the mine was pretty stale, so he didn't see many. Maybe the flooding in the slope was pushing more air this way. If it didn't actually close off the ventilation, they'd have better air until the pumps got fixed.

Liam followed the coal car down the tracks. His stomach rumbled again, and he frowned. He had another mile to walk just to get to the coal room where his father was waiting. It was a better room than their last one. He had hated that monkey hole. He'd had to crawl and climb the last quarter mile.

Liam kept walking, stooping his shoulders as the ceiling got lower. He hoped Nolan could go fishing on Sunday. He imagined being out in the crisp, fresh air for a moment, then pushed the thought aside. Sunday was a long ways off.

CHAPTER TWO

Rory dumped the bucket of water into the iron cauldron that hung in the washroom hearth. As she straightened and pushed her hair back off her forehead, she heard the steam whistle call the miners to dinner. She set down the bucket. "Is that enough?"

Her mother glanced up from the steaming laundry tub. "One more." She gestured with the laundry paddle. "And bring your washboard on the way back. You can use the small tub."

Rory picked up the bucket and swung it in a wide arc as she turned.

"Rory!"

"What?" Rory faced her mother.

"You know what. We are this close to losing

our house." She held up her hand, a tiny space between her thumb and forefinger. "I can't pay for a repair of the window, or buy another bucket if you break it against the wall. If the Quinns decided to board elsewhere, I don't know how we'd get by."

"With my bakery wages—" Rory began.

"Your wages help, Rory," Mama said, sighing. "But we don't have a penny saved and we have so much on tick at the store that I'm afraid they'll stop putting things on credit for us. All it'll take is some fool accident and we could lose the house. Is that what you want?"

Rory glared at her mother for a few seconds, then lowered her head, mumbling an apology. Then, careful to keep the bucket so close that the edge of her apron draped around it, she went out the washroom door and closed it behind her, hard.

"Don't slam that door," she heard her mother call in an exasperated voice.

"Sorry," Rory yelled. Then she lifted her chin and swung the bucket in a complete circle, spinning around with it, feeling the pale sunshine warm her skin.

The pump was just past the garden patch. She set the bucket down and worked the handle up and down, leaning her full weight on it at first. The water came in ragged gushes that splattered her face and arms. She stopped pumping as it neared the top of the bucket, then stood still, leaning against the side of the house.

The day was cool. It wouldn't be that long before the weather turned cold. The blue-gray cabbages in the garden were heavy and round. First frost, two weeks before, had mellowed the bitter leaves. Mama didn't want to bring them in before she had to, though. They would spoil faster in the pantry than out here.

The sound of coughing made Rory look across the picket fence into the Tellers' yard. "You all right, then, Mr. Teller?"

The old man waved one hand at her, half-turning as he doubled over, his breathing labored. Rory watched him closely. If need be, she would jump the fence to pound on his back. She glanced toward the washroom door. Her mother would be wondering what was taking so long.

Mr. Teller finally took a handkerchief from his pocket and pressed it against his lips. "Weather taking a turn for winter, isn't it?" he said after a moment. "Cold last night."

Rory nodded. "Haven't seen you out for a while, Mr. Teller."

He nodded, an exaggerated motion. She could hear him still clearing his throat, swallowing, trying not to have another coughing spasm.

"I'm supposed to be helping Mama wash," she said.

He nodded again, the handkerchief tight against his mouth now, his eyes watering. Rory smiled at him and slipped her hand through the bucket bale, careful not to slop water onto her dress or the hem of her apron. She glanced at him and smiled once more, walking back toward the washroom. Reluctantly, she pulled the door open and went inside.

"Where's your washboard, Rory?"

Rory set the bucket down, frowning. "I forgot. It's out by the outhouse where I scrubbed Paddy's shirt."

Her mother was staring at her. "So go get it. The work won't do itself, Rory."

Banging the door, Rory managed a smile at Mr. Teller as she passed the garden, then turned the corner into the backyard. She had left her washboard standing against the fence.

"Rory, girl! And how are you?"

She looked up. Mrs. Dover was standing next to a stout willow basket filled with clean laundry. She had a damp sheet over one arm. "Did you hear about the pumps failing last night?"

Rory shook her head, her stomach tightening.

"Only for a few hours, I am told, but John says any more water down in his section and they will have to relocate. I am wondering if he shouldn't just go talk to the operator out at the Hickory colliery, or maybe go see if the Jackson is hiring."

Rory nodded, not wanting to say anything that would keep Mrs. Dover talking. She didn't want to hear about the mines, about the flooding, about who was hiring and who wasn't. Her father and her brother were dead and gone—

and there would be no more miners in her family, ever.

"I saw you out here yesterday. Washing on a Sunday?" Mrs. Dover arched her eyebrows and waited for Rory to speak.

"Paddy got a nosebleed. I just did the one shirt for him."

"Paddy's the sickly one?"

Rory shook her head. "Not sickly, just too much breaker dust and—"

"Some can take it, others can't," Mrs. Dover said curtly. "My boys all worked in the breaker when they were small and all four of them are down in the mines now. Never a day sick with any of them. Never a one hurt in the mines."

Rory closed her eyes for a second.

"I'm sorry, dear," Mrs. Dover said quickly. "I wasn't thinking."

Rory hugged her washboard against her chest. "Paddy's fine, anyway," she said to change the subject. "He's coughing yet, but the fever is gone."

"Has his father tried making him up an asafetida bag?"

Rory shook her head. "I don't think so."

Mrs. Dover laughed. "Oh, you'd have noticed. The gum smells to high heaven. But I have a sister down in West Virginia who swears by it."

"Rory!"

She turned at the sound of her mother's voice. "I have to go."

Mrs. Dover walked toward her clothesline, lifting the damp sheet. "Don't get into trouble. You run along."

Rory hurried back into the washroom. "I'm sorry, Mama. Mrs. Dover was out hanging laundry," she said before her mother could scold her.

"That woman has entirely too much time on her hands. Three grown daughters and no boarders to cook and clean for. She probably has time to sit and read a book or knit." Mama fell back into the steady rhythm of scrubbing, the soapy water sloshing gently against the side of her tub.

"Mrs. Dover said the pumps failed last night."

Mama stopped again and looked up. "No concern of ours."

"But, Mama—"

"Rory, the only good thing about your father and brother dying down there is that I don't have to live in fear of it anymore."

Rory pulled her wash stool from its hook on the wall. She leaned over the small tub, setting the feet of her washboard solidly against the bottom. Then she reached out and pulled a pair of coal-stained work pants from the pile of dirty clothes and set to work, the lye soap stinging her hands.

Liam shoveled the last bit of coal onto the car, stacking it a little higher. The foreman had told them all not to stint the loads, that Kirk and Baum had warned against light loads or using rubble to line the bottom of the cars. Liam tagged the load with his father's name and number, then pushed it slowly out to the siding where a driver could see it easily.

The sound of a blast farther up the tunnel made Liam pause. There had been blasts every half hour or so. Whoever was working up there was using a lot of powder. They had either hit very hard coal or someone had drilled badly placed holes.

"Liam!"

"Da? You need me?"

"Come on up, boy," came his father's shout.

Liam scrambled over the slick coal, following the vein upward at an angle. His father was still lying on his side, half hidden by the shelf of coal he was digging beneath. Da had been in that position for two hours, holding his head up to aim his light. Sprags braced the face, holding it up from below, the stout sticks jammed into the cut his father had made. It was a deep undercut. It was going to drop a ton or more, Liam was sure.

"I've just about got this finished, Liam," Da said. "Did you get a full load out of that last?"

"I did," Liam told him.

"I'm thinking to ask the foreman if we can put Paddy into a trapper's spot. I know Donegal's boy is about to leave his post for a driver's job."

"That'd be good," Liam agreed.

His father didn't answer, but the steady clinking of his pick on the coal resumed, and Liam knew the matter was settled in his father's mind. Liam picked up his flat shovel again. Pitching coal down the steep tunnel, he stopped only when he had to catch his breath. His father worked just as steadily, cutting into the hard coal with perfectly aimed blows. Undercutting too far could mean being crushed by a premature fall. But too shallow a cut would only have to be deepened later.

Liam knew his father preferred not to blast unless he had to. It was safer by far to use a pick and careful craftsmanship. Once the last bit of loose coal was shoveled down the chute, Liam turned back and watched his father.

To be a miner—one of the men who came out of the tunnel every day, tired but proud—that was the only thing Liam had ever wanted in his life. And once he and Da were both mining, they could use Paddy and a hired man to load. Then they would make real money. Then, they could send for Colleen, Shannon, and

Fiona. He missed his sisters. But after Ma had died of the quick fever, there had been no choice but to send them to Aunt Mary's.

A rumbling in the rock overhead stilled his thoughts and forced him to look upward. It lasted only a few seconds, but he imagined the weight of the earth pressing down on the timbers that braced the sides of the tunnel. Da had said they were about 400 feet down here. As the odd grinding sound stopped, Liam realized he was holding his breath, and exhaled.

He glanced toward his father. Da had stopped working but hadn't rolled from beneath the overhang. When the noise in the rock overhead subsided, the steady sound of his pick began again.

CHAPTER THREE

Rory sat on the porch, staring up at the stars. Liam and Paddy were in the front room, still whooping and celebrating over the news their father had brought. Paddy was going to leave the breaker and become a trapper boy. They were all so excited, it was like Christmastide, as though the supervisor had given Paddy a wonderful gift.

Rory shook her head. All she wanted was to leave St. Claire. If she never saw a culm pile or a breaker again, it'd be too soon.

The door banged open, and Paddy came out, grinning. "Rory? There you are! Did you hear? Did you?"

Rory nodded, trying to smile. "I did."

"I'm going underground!" His voice was soft and full of wonder, his thin shoulders squared. "Da says Mama would have been proud," he breathed.

"I am sure she would have been," Rory agreed, forcing a second smile.

"I've been doing well enough on the breaker," he said, hooking his thumbs into his waistband. He looked like a small version of Liam, and Rory felt her smile widen. Paddy never complained, even though he had more to complain about than most. He ducked his head to cough, then grinned. "Now we can send another dollar or two a week to the girls."

Rory saw the pride in his eyes and wondered if his sisters loved him as much as he loved them. "They are lucky little girls to have brothers like you and Liam."

He seemed to grow an inch or two taller. "This means Colleen can have her new dress for school."

Liam came out onto the porch. "Da says you are to get straight to your cot," he told Paddy. "Your first day will be long enough without you being sleepy."

Without answering, Paddy ran down the porch steps and put his arms out, spinning in a circle. "No more slate picking for me!" he shouted.

Liam laughed, and Rory couldn't help but smile at how happy they were. Paddy came up the steps, coughing, his eyes sparkling in the faint light from the front room lantern. "I bet I get up before you tomorrow, Liam."

Liam shook his head and lifted one hand, pretending that he was about to cuff his brother. Paddy dodged away, feigning fear. He bolted back through the door. Liam laughed again, then turned to face Rory. "I wondered where you ran off to."

Rory looked up at him. "I didn't want to spoil anything."

"You thinking about Andrew and your father?"

Rory shook her head, then gave in. "Probably."

Liam sat down by her, and she slid over to make room for him on the step. "Paddy will make more money as a trapper boy, and it's a lot safer, Rory."

Rory shot him a look. "Nothing is safe down there."

"Paddy is nearly eleven and he's—"

"He's a sweet-natured boy with a weak constitution," Rory interrupted. "And you and your father are killing him by putting him underground."

Liam frowned. "Those are harsh words, Rory."

She nodded. "But it's true, and you know it."

He frowned. "Underground will be better. There's dust, but not nearly so bad as the breaker. And he won't be bent in half all day."

Rory sighed. "Unless the ceiling falls on him, he'll be just fine."

"So what should we do?" Liam demanded, standing up. "Da already sends most of our money to my aunt so she can keep the girls for us."

Rory shook her head, her eyes stinging. "I don't know. I hate the mines, that's all."

"Not everyone gets hurt, Rory."

She met his eyes. "No, the lucky ones get miner's lung. Mr. Teller can barely walk around his yard."

Liam wasn't listening. He was staring up into the sky, his back toward her.

"Liam?"

He turned. "What?"

"Don't you ever think about getting away from the mines?"

He looked at her. "Get away? I'm going to be as good a miner as my Da. Maybe better."

Rory shook her head. "No, I mean it. Don't you ever just dream of doing something else?"

Liam shrugged. "What? Farming? They work as hard or harder than we do, Da says."

"Anything," Rory snapped at him. "Selling buttons, being in a circus—"

"Gold mining, maybe," Liam interrupted her. "There was that big strike out in Colorado last year and—"

"Mining!" Rory interrupted. "It's all you can think about. You remind me of my brother."

"I'm sorry about your Da and Andrew," Liam said slowly and carefully. "But nothing like that is going to happen to Paddy."

"You can't be sure of that." Rory stood up and went down the porch steps and across the yard, scuffing her feet in the dust. She could hear Mill Creek, rushing between its bricked banks down along First Street. With all the collieries in production, it would be running black.

She heard the door open and shut and turned in time to see Liam disappear inside. He was angry with her, and she didn't blame him. But she couldn't stand the thought of Paddy down in the black maze that ran under half the streets in town. Sighing, she went back inside. "I'm going to bed if you don't need help," she called to her mother.

"No, Rory, I'm about finished," her mother answered from the kitchen.

Rory opened their bedroom door and went in, pulling the curtain that separated her bed from her mother's. She heard the clock strike midnight before she finally went to sleep.

In the morning, Rory thought Paddy's cough was worse, but he ate his oatmeal and bacon. Liam sat beside him at the table. Mama stood at the worktable, filling dinner tins.

"Rory?"

She turned from the stove to look at Paddy.

"Da says when a boy goes underground he's on his way to being a man."

"That's right." Mr. Quinn caught Rory's eye. "Is there a bit more of that bacon, lass?"

Rory used a pot rag to carry the skillet to the table. Mr. Quinn speared three fat slices with his knife, then slid one onto Liam's plate and another onto Paddy's, saving the third for himself.

"Rory, will you bring in an onion for me, please?" Mama asked from the worktable. The dinner tins were set out before her in a neat row. "Take the candle lantern."

Rory set the skillet back on the iron stove top. She hung the pot rag on its hook and picked up the lantern, then headed for the back door. The washroom had been swept out. Rory smiled. Liam always saved her from a little work if he could. Or maybe it had been Paddy. He had taken the last bath the night before. The tub was hanging up as it should be, and the square of brown soap was high and dry on the shelf.

Rory pushed open the washroom door. It

was still nearly dark. There was a chilly breeze blowing, and the candle flickered a little inside its glass box. The shovel was leaning against the side of the house. Rory set the lantern on the dirt and lifted her skirt as she began to dig.

The ground was hard from the summer's rains, and she had to dig carefully; Mama would be furious if she cut a good onion in half. Turning the earth, she reached down and picked up the fat bulb she had displaced. Brushing dirt off the papery skin, she leaned down for the lantern again, then went in.

"Cut it up, please," Mama said as Rory closed the door behind herself.

"Get an extra shirt on, Paddy," Mr. Quinn was saying as Rory went to the sink to wash the onion. Paddy stood. A few seconds later she heard his footsteps on the circular stair.

"We could be a bit late tonight," Mr. Quinn announced. "A few of the boys wanted to toast Paddy's welcome underground."

"I'll keep the stew hot for you," Mama said.

Liam rose, scraping his chair back. He started to pick up his dirty dishes, but his father gestured and he set them down. "Get a move on, Liam. We're already a little late. The boss won't like that on Paddy's first day."

"Rory," Mama said. "I need onion for their sandwiches so I can close up the tins."

The knives were beside the drain board. Rory skinned the onion, looking up when Paddy came back into the kitchen, walking like a little rooster, his cap set almost sideways and his eyes lit from within.

Rory cut the onion in half, then began to slice it, the pungent fumes rising to sting her eyes. Mama scooped up the thin white slices with her broad-bladed knife. She laid them in even layers on the cold slabs of mutton, then slid the tin lids into place.

Rory kept glancing at Paddy as he waited, warming himself by the iron stove. She didn't let the tears stream down her face until Paddy had followed his father and brother out the front door and into the darkness.

CHAPTER FOUR

"Where are you off to?" Liam heard Nolan shout.

"Thought I'd run up to see Paddy for a moment," Liam answered, turning to look back up the tunnel.

"He's been at the door almost a week now, hasn't he?" Nolan said as the coal car drew closer. Liam nodded and slowed, falling into step beside Lucky. The mule acknowledged him with a quick blast of warm breath against his cheek, but she was too smart to slow even a little on the gradual incline that led back toward the shaft.

"I see him every trip," Nolan said. "He's all right."

Liam walked alongside, expecting more, but Nolan only pressed his lips together and stared ahead as the car rumbled along the narrow tracks.

"Thought I'd just make sure he's eating his dinner and all," Liam said.

Nolan nodded, looking at him sidelong. "You got pie again today?"

Liam hesitated, then nodded. "Apple."

Nolan whistled between his teeth. "My ma will nearly never bake a pie. Says it's too much work."

"It's my landlady's daughter who bakes them. She's so good at it, they hire her down at Schumacher's bakery two days a week."

"My ma says that we're lucky to be fed at all the way the little ones take all her time."

"Maybe when the twins are older," Liam said. "My mother used to say that babies are more work than a man can ever know."

Nolan shrugged. "A pie once in a while couldn't be that hard to manage."

His voice was so sad, so full of longing, that Liam gave in. "If you want a little piece of mine, I'll save it for you."

Nolan snapped to attention. "You would? Liam, if you would do that for me, I would—"

"Just keep an eye on Paddy, will you? If you see him slouching or getting sleepy—"

"I'll let you know," Nolan promised. "He was all right last trip in. Just that cough."

"And if you hear any of the rougher drivers planning a trick on him—"

"I'll do what I can, but he'll probably get a dinner or two stolen, maybe get spun around in circles and have to wander a bit while they have their laugh."

"Just so nobody hurts him," Liam said. "He's a lot tougher than he looks, but he's pretty young, Nolan."

"He'll be fine enough, Liam. They never keep it up for long unless the boy cries and whines." Nolan smiled. "You worry too much. This is where I turn."

Liam nodded as Nolan spoke to Lucky. The mule veered southward, following another line of track. Liam waved. As the coal car rumbled away, he kept on down the gangway toward the shaft. He pitied the miners down where Nolan had headed. That was the bad patch; they were probably knee-deep in water.

Liam was glad Da had refused to work down there, even with the extra pay for pillar robbing. The uneven passages in that section connected low-lying coal rooms that were partly flooded but still being worked. Da said Kirk and Baum had to get every lump of coal they could to pay back the cost of all the improvements they'd made. The slope they'd dug had been expensive, and the connecting tunnels that led up to the Seven-Foot Vein had taken a few months to complete.

It seemed to Liam that it had been worth it—the ventilation was a lot better. The miners all said that Kirk and Baum were hoping to do what McGuinness hadn't been able to do: make the St. Claire colliery pay.

A group of men carrying braces came out of a passage just in front of Liam. The stout, heavy timbers required three men each, and even then the men had to walk slowly.

Liam stood tall, like the lord of the manor, nudging his cap into a rakish angle. "Right up there, gentlemen," he called to them. "My Da's name is—"

"Get off it, Irish. These are for the gangway, just over there."

"And I thought you were wanting to make sure I had no worries."

The men laughed, shuffling past him, maneuvering the long posts to the far side of the gangway.

"You hear the roof working?" one of the men shouted back at Liam.

"Yesterday," he called back. "Just one long rumble. Nothing since."

"They're talking about some noise this morning on the east side of the Seven-Foot Vein, close to the slope. Just wondered if you'd heard it down here," the man said.

Liam shook his head and turned. Da would have today's second face down soon, and it would be time for him to load again. Stopping once to check his miner's lamp, Liam walked as fast as he could. He had to keep to the side; every few minutes a mule driver went past.

The section of gangway where Paddy was working was quiet except for the sound of dripping water. Feathery wreaths of fungus grew out of the support timbers, draping the old wood. The air seemed stale, heavy, and damp. It was colder here as well—the newest trapper boys always got the worst stations.

Liam came through the door after shouting for an all clear. Paddy answered quick and sharp, but then Liam heard him cough.

"Aw, you didn't need to come all this way," Paddy said as he shoved the door closed again and turned around.

Liam looked him over. Paddy was wearing his jacket buttoned high beneath his chin. The cheese crate that served him as a seat was scooted back from the rails. Beside it lay a stick of wood, sharpened at one end.

"Whittling?" Liam asked.

Paddy nodded somberly. "There's a driver who has taught his mule to bite."

Liam started to get angry, but then he saw Paddy's grin and glanced again at the sharpened sprag. "Remember that it's not the mule that deserves the poke."

"I will," Paddy promised.

Liam reached out to grasp Paddy's shoulder. "You all right, then?"

"Sure I am. You go on back. Da needs . . ." Paddy cleared his throat, then turned to one side as he began to cough.

The sound of it sickened Liam. He stood uneasily, waiting until the long convulsion of coughing ended. "You shouldn't be down here."

"Where else would I be, Liam?"

"Back at Mrs. Hamilton's, letting Rory fuss over you with tea and soup, getting well."

Paddy shook his head. "We can't afford to lose my wage, and you know it. And it isn't just the day or two I am talking about."

Liam understood his brother perfectly. If Paddy had to take time off this soon after being allowed to start as a trapper boy, the mine boss would find someone else. And when Paddy was well enough to come back, he would likely be told there was no longer a position open. There were dozens of boys who wanted to get out of the breaker.

"Stay warm as you can," Liam said, finally.

"Get up and move around some and don't start any wars with the mule drivers. Just take whatever they do with a stone face, and they'll get bored soon enough."

Paddy nodded and started coughing again. Liam waited, glancing at the door, wondering how Paddy could hear the coal cars coming in the middle of a coughing fit. Feeling the weight of worry on his shoulders, Liam bid Paddy farewell and started back up the gangway.

Rory dipped the rag into the bucket. The soapy water was already black. She wrung the cloth out, then turned back to the front windowsill. Mama was strict as death on coal dust, and Rory was glad. Some people's houses were thick with it all the time. Mrs. Dover's place was terrible. Even her kitchen table was gritty with the fine, black powder.

A muted thump startled Rory, and she stared at the floor. They were blasting down in the mine, somewhere close. Since Kirk and Baum had bought the mine from Mr. McGuinness and sunk the new slope, the works had expanded rapidly. Mr. Quinn said there were a lot more miners being hired. He was hoping the new owners with their big plans would mean the St. Claire colliery would thrive. Rory hoped the whole thing would flood and shut down the way it had a few years before.

"Rory!"

"What, Mama?"

"Come give me a hand, will you?"

Rory plopped her rag into the bucket and went into the front room. Mama's voice was coming from upstairs. She was changing the Quinns' bed linens today. Tomorrow they would beat rugs and wash the floors. Rory started up the stairs, following the half circle as the steps curved.

Mama was standing next to Paddy's cot. "Look at this."

Rory edged to see down along the wall where her mother had pulled the cot out. There were two or three dozen rags, crumpled into wads.

"What . . . ?" Rory asked, puzzled. A second later she understood.

"It's that cough of his," Mama was saying. "I

wondered where the rags were going. He's been stealing them and cutting them up to use as handkerchiefs."

Rory frowned. "But why wouldn't he just let us wash them and—"

"Because he's hiding it, Rory," Mama cut her off. "His father sleeps like a rotting log and probably hasn't any idea how sick that child is. He's going to die of pneumonia if they aren't careful."

Rory's stomach tightened. "He's not that sick, Mama. He just—"

"He's a brave lad, and I like him, too, Rory, but it's none of our worry. Take these down and just burn them in the stove."

Rory nodded, bending to gather up the little wads of cloth. As she straightened, she heard a sharp rapping on the front door.

"Go see who it is, Rory," Mama said. "Then get back to cleaning, will you?"

Rory went back down the steps, running into the kitchen to pitch the crumpled cloths into the stove firebox. Then she ran to the door.

"Ah, you are home," Mrs. Schumacher said as Rory opened the door.

Rory looked past her. Mr. Schumacher had stopped the carriage in the middle of the street and was waiting. "Is everything all right, Mrs. Schumacher?"

"My sister up in Ashland is ill, Rory. Mr. Schumacher and I are going up for a week or so to see if we can help. The bakery will be closed."

Rory stared at her. "I could come in and make the pies, anyway, and . . ."

Mrs. Schumacher raised a hand to silence her. "No, no, dear. We can't be sure when we'll be back and we don't want to be worrying about the bakery while we're gone."

Rory tried to think of something to say. Mama depended on her bakery wages—without them, they would soon be short of food and coal. But before Rory could speak, Mrs. Schumacher had turned away and was hurrying toward the carriage. Rory stood on the porch and watched them until the birch trees at the corner of Hancock hid them from view. Then she stamped her foot.

The Schumachers owned seven houses in town that they rented to miners' families. The bakery was only part of their income—and a small part at that. They had talked about closing it the year before; then, with the new owners at the St. Claire talking about expanding the mine, they had decided to stay open.

Rory caught one last glimpse of the carriage as it turned down Hancock. If Mrs. Schumacher's sister didn't get better soon, there was no telling how long they would be gone.

"Rory? Who was it?"

Rory spun around. Mama was standing at the foot of the stairs with her hands on her hips. "Was it that insurance salesman again? Mrs. Dover says he's been going right into the mine, trying to sell policies to the working men."

Rory shook her head, thinking furiously. She didn't want to upset Mama if she didn't have to. Maybe she could pick up a few days' work somewhere in town if she spent time tomorrow going from shop to shop. Sometimes the store-keepers would hire a sweeper or pay to have their windows washed. She would find something. She just had to.

"Rory? Did you hear me?"

"It was Mrs. Schumacher," Rory said.

"Has she changed your schedule again?"

"Yes," Rory said, feeling a stab of guilt at lying to her mother. "But it won't matter much. I go tomorrow."

"That's good, then," Mama said. She pointed at the bucket. "About time to change the water, Rory, or you'll just be spreading the coal dust around."

Rory nodded, then Mama was gone. She stared back down the street, wondering what she was going to do.

CHAPTER FIVE

Rory watched Paddy push his plate away. He was leaning on one elbow, and his face was paler than usual except for two bright spots of pink high on his cheeks.

"Eat up, boy," Mr. Quinn admonished him.

"Leave him be, Da." Liam was frowning.

Paddy shook his head and stood up. "I'm going to bed, Da."

They all sat in silence after Paddy left. Rory heard the slow thudding of his footsteps on the stairs, then the all-too-familiar sound of his cough.

"My wife used to make a mustard plaster," Mr. Quinn said, looking at Mama.

She shook her head. "That boy needs sleep, food, and rest more than he needs a mustard plaster."

"I can't have him miss work," Mr. Quinn said softly.

"He'll lose his position if he does," Liam added. Rory could see the worry on his face.

"I can make a plaster," Mama said, pushing back her chair. "Mr. Quinn, if you give me a hand at the pestle, it'll go faster. Or Liam?"

"Liam, you finish supper," Mr. Quinn said, standing. They went into the kitchen, and Rory heard her mother taking down the heavy iron boiling pot and sliding it across the stove top.

"I'd give anything to keep him out of that mine for a few days," Liam whispered, lifting his chin to gesture upstairs.

Rory nodded sympathetically. Paddy had been so proud, and she knew as well as anyone the difference a few dollars a week could make. A sudden, piercing memory of Andrew made Rory's heart ache. She could remember him swaggering along, thrilled as anything when Papa had bought him his first man-sized pick.

"It just seemed like things were starting to get better for us," Liam whispered. Rory nodded again.

"I wish we could have one of the other boys take over for a week or so," Liam said quietly, as if he was talking to himself. "But there's not a single lad in this town who wouldn't try to keep the position once the week was up. I would ask one of the old-timers, but most of them are crippled-up or worse."

"Trapper boy is an easy job, isn't it?"

Liam looked at her. "Sure. But it's almost a mile in, and that's a long walk for someone with coal lung or a bad leg. And besides, someone might notice and maybe tell the boss."

"Would he care?"

Liam shrugged. "Maybe, maybe not. He wouldn't like us pulling a switch without saying something."

Rory watched him lower his head, rubbing his face with both hands. His shoulders sagged, and for a second she could see how tired he was. A mile, she thought, picturing Paddy walking that distance every morning, coughing, struggling to keep up. "Poor Paddy," she said aloud.

"It's murder down there for him right now," Liam agreed. "It's cold and damp where he is— probably the worst door on that gangway, but he's the newest and . . ."

An idea was forming in Rory's mind as Liam trailed off. She shivered, knowing she had to at least consider it. She met Liam's eyes. "Would the boy get Paddy's pay?"

Liam sat up straighter. "Do you know someone we could trust? This is Paddy's job. I won't have him going back to that breaker for anyone."

"I know someone," Rory answered. Then she hesitated. "Maybe."

Liam leaned toward her. "It can't be anyone too tall, or someone would notice. I want to keep this on the sly."

The eagerness in his voice let Rory know that it was really up to her. He was desperate. She pulled in a long breath. Could she do it? It might easily make the difference between Mama losing the house and keeping it. At the very least it would save her weeks of sleepless worry.

"Is it someone I know?" Liam asked anxiously.

Rory took in another breath. Her father had gone down in that mine every day for years to keep this house. She closed her eyes for a moment, then opened them to find Liam staring at her. "The bakery is closing for a week or maybe more," Rory told him. "Mrs. Schumacher's sister is sick."

Liam was silent for a minute or more. Then his eyes widened. "You mean you?"

Rory laced her fingers together so that he couldn't see that her hands were shaking. "Why not? Mama depends on my wage, and it'd do you a favor."

Liam sat back. "That's crazy. You know how most miners feel about women underground. They'd skin me alive if they found out."

Rory tried not to imagine what it would be like in the dark gangway. Telling Mama that she wasn't going to earn her wage for a week or more would be almost as bad. "I can wear a hat. No one will know."

Liam stared at her. "I hope it'll only be for a day or two."

"Would your Da let me? Or does he believe women are bad luck underground?"

Liam thought a moment, then shook his head. "Da's not that superstitious. But maybe it's better he doesn't know."

"I'd have to hide it from Mama."

Abruptly, Liam shook his head. "It's a bad idea, Rory."

Rory fell silent. If Mama found out, she would forbid it even though she was going to be desperate about losing the week's wages at the bakery. Rory wanted to believe there was some other way to earn money—but there probably wasn't. Even if she found shopkeepers to hire her, a sweeper's wage wasn't much.

"A girl your age isn't safe in the mine, Rory," Liam was saying. "The men are rough, and they curse and—"

Rory shook her head. That wasn't what she was worried about. "Are you forgetting that my father and brother were coal miners, Liam? Besides, I'd dress like a boy, and no one would know."

Liam didn't answer, and Rory could tell he was thinking about it. A chill spread outward from her belly. What if he said yes?

"Here we are," Mama said from the kitchen door. She had the meat platter covered with a thick towel, and the steam rising from its edges carried the sharp, irritating odor of boiled mustard seed. "You just place it square on his chest," Mama explained to Mr. Quinn as she passed the platter to him. Then she turned to Rory. "Let's get that kitchen cleaned up for the evening."

Liam leaned forward, pushing his chair back. As he stood he bent close to Rory's ear. "Don't tell anyone. I'll make up something for Da. Be up an hour before daybreak, just like you would for the bakery. I'll bring Paddy's clothes."

Then he was stretching, following his father upstairs. Rory could only sit and watch him go. It was done. She couldn't back out now.

★　★　★

Liam was frantic to get going. Paddy had gone back to sleep as soon as they had told him he didn't have to work.

"Are you sure, son?" Da asked for the third time as they sat at breakfast.

Liam nodded, avoiding even a quick glance at Rory. "I talked to the boy yesterday, Da. He's willing to do it for three or four days, or a week—and expects no more than Paddy's pay."

Da shoveled in another huge mouthful of fried ham, and Liam waited, hoping he wouldn't ask who was going to take the job.

"How long at the bakery today?" Mrs. Hamilton asked Rory. Liam heard Rory take in a quick breath, and he was careful not to look at her as she answered.

"All day today. Perhaps even later than usual."

Mama stopped stirring the oatmeal. "If Mrs. Schumacher is throwing out any week-old loaves, bring a few home, will you? We can dry the crumbs for pudding."

"Yes, Mama," Liam heard Rory mumble. He stuffed down another few bites, then stood up, still chewing.

"I have to leave a bit early to go meet Paddy's replacement, Da. Will you carry my dinner tin? I'll meet you down below."

Da nodded and tipped his plate to soak the ham grease into his biscuit. "I'm going on down. Get started early today."

Liam pretended to reach for the salt dish, breathing a whisper so faint, he was afraid Rory might not hear him. "I'll wait for you on Carroll Street."

She nodded, almost imperceptibly.

Liam leaned back, allowing himself one quick glance at Rory. Then he jutted his chin out, tipping his head a fraction of an inch before he turned and strode out of the room.

Paddy's clothes were in a neat pile in their clothespress, and Liam scooped them up. He hurried down the stairs, called out a good-bye, and didn't pause until he was out the front door.

He crossed Third Street almost running and went down a half block, then stepped into a thick copse of birch trees near the corner of Carroll. Ducking into the low branches he settled himself against one of the smooth, white tree trunks and waited in the dusky predawn light.

It wasn't long before Da went past. Liam pressed himself against the tree, holding his breath. Da was whistling, swinging the dinner tins as he strode along. Liam held himself motionless until his father turned up Carroll Street toward the breaker.

Liam exhaled. This was a piece of luck. Da would already be up in the room working before Rory took her place at the door—he'd never even see her. Liam listened carefully. Finally, light footsteps told him Rory was coming. When she appeared out of the murk, she was walking slowly, looking from side to side. He waited until she was close. "Psssst!"

She jumped, startled, then looked both ways before she came into the birch trees.

"Are you sure you want to do this?" Liam asked, afraid she might back out, but knowing he had to give her the chance. There was a long silence, and he braced himself, but then she sighed.

"I have to."

"Here are the clothes." He handed her the bundle, then walked out into the street and stood guard with his back to the birch trees. "No one's coming," he whispered over his shoulder. "Hurry and we might not run into anyone."

There were rustling sounds, and then a low-voiced exclamation. A moment later, he heard her come out of the trees.

"What do you think?" she asked.

He turned around, peering at her in the dark. She had tucked her hair beneath Paddy's cap. The shirt seemed to fit her fine. He took a step backward, squinting. The trousers were a little long, but that was common enough among the younger boys. Most of them wore hand-me-downs. He nodded as she put on the jacket. "Some coal dust on your face and I think you'll be fine. The drivers won't say much at first. You're beneath them. Stay clear of the mules. A few of them kick or bite. If anyone teases or plays a prank, just stay quiet and don't cry."

Rory grimaced. "Will they?"

"They haven't got much time to spare during the workday, and I'll walk back with you so you don't get lost." He put his hand on her shoulder and felt her shivering. He started to ask her if she still wanted to take Paddy's place, but he held his tongue. If she *was* having second thoughts, what would he do? Let Paddy lose his job when someone noticed the door wasn't tended?

Liam looked past her. "Your clothes all right here?"

"I hid them under a pile of leaves."

Liam nodded briskly, ignoring the noticeable unsteadiness in her voice. He started walking toward the shaft, and she followed.

CHAPTER SIX

Rory hesitated at the top of the ladder. She could feel her own heartbeat, and her mouth was dry. The miner's lamp on her cap felt odd and heavy. Liam had lit his own, then hers, tucking a box of matches into her pocket. The flat, tin reflector behind the wick protected the cap from catching fire. But it was still strange to think that a little flame was burning within inches of her hair.

"I'll go first," Liam said, gripping her shoulder. "Just don't look down."

The sound of the shaft engine was painfully loud as a cage went upward, passing them. Liam gripped the sides of the ladder and started downward. The sound of raucous voices distracted Rory, and she looked up. A group of men appeared out of the dusk and started toward them. Rory swallowed hard.

"Come on," Liam insisted, his head level with her feet. Then he disappeared, climbing downward. Rory stepped onto the first rung, then looked down into the inkwell blackness below her. She could barely see Liam. The voices above her were coming closer. She could hear the men laughing. Shaking, afraid the approaching men would see that she was a girl, she started down the ladder. The men came closer, then stopped, talking.

Rory drew in a long breath and tried to concentrate on going down the ladder. The rungs were worn smooth, and she wished she had rubber boots. Her own shoes were slick-soled. She placed her feet carefully, counting, telling herself she wouldn't look until she was sure she was close to the bottom. Once or twice she felt Liam touch her ankle, a quick, reassuring pressure. She kept counting. At 150, she allowed herself a glance, leaning out just a little to see better.

Below her she saw what looked like fireflies on a summer night—except that the tiny, faraway lights were traveling in straighter lines. Miners' lamps, she realized, and a sweat sprang out on her brow.

She looked up. The men were still standing near the top. She could hear their voices and see the distant flickering of their lights. As she stared upward, the ladder suddenly jolted beneath her hands. Someone was starting down. After a few seconds, she could see a dim outline. The man was moving fast.

"Rory! Come on!"

She stepped onto the next rung and pinched Liam's fingers.

"Ouch!"

Rory looked down, bending to apologize, then glanced up when the ladder began to shake again. Six or seven men were descending in a tight column, moving faster down the rungs than she would have imagined was possible. She felt a tug at her trouser leg and started downward, acutely aware of her sweating palms and the smooth wood beneath them.

Rory forced herself to step from one rung to the next as quickly as she dared, scared to look up or down, focusing her eyes on the wooden planks that lined the shaft wall behind the ladder. The rungs slipped past like a picket fence, endless, dizzying.

The men above closed the distance rapidly, and Rory descended frantically, her hands automatically judging the span of the rungs, her heart pounding as the heavy boots came closer.

The last step onto solid rock drove a shock through her whole body, and Rory pitched backward. She would have fallen flat, but Liam caught her awkwardly and set her back on her feet as the derisive laughter of the men rang out.

"Not quite used to the ladder yet, eh lad?" one of them asked, setting off another round of guffaws. Liam grabbed Rory's arm and turned her away. Their catcalls and jeers rose as she stumbled over the iron car tracks. Liam steadied her again and helped her stay upright.

"Watch your footing," he said, just loudly enough for her to hear.

She tried. The lamp weighted her cap, and it kept sliding askew. She reached to straighten it and felt the quick heat of the flame. Liam marched her to a recess in the glittery black wall of the tunnel and held her still, facing it, as the men went by, laughing. Rory wrinkled her nose, realizing that this was what her father had called "a gob pile." There were no trash barrels or outhouses in the mines.

"I'm sorry," she said as soon as the men were well past. She looked up at Liam and was surprised at how different his face looked lit only by the light that rose above his cap. His eyes seemed sunken, his cheeks too prominent.

"I'm not sure you can do this," he said in a low voice.

"I can," Rory interrupted him. Her legs were still shaky, but she wasn't sure if it was from fear or anger. She hated the man who had nearly stepped on her hands, forcing her down the ladder.

Rory tried to calm herself. Her brother probably had had to put up with men like that, at least at first. He had been nine years old when he had gone into the mines with Papa. And she had never heard Liam or Paddy complain.

"Are you all right?" Liam asked.

"Yes." Rory squared her shoulders. She looked down the tunnel. It was narrower than she had thought.

Liam walked toward a rough wooden bench lined with safety lanterns. He lit two and handed her one. Rory was grateful for the extra light as he started off, leading her down the gangway the men had taken. He followed a path that ran alongside the car rails. Bits and chunks of coal littered the ground. Rory could feel the grit scraping against the thin soles of her shoes.

There were thick, round timbers jammed between the floor and the ceiling. Some of them were bent, like giant knees. Rory walked past them, lifting her lantern higher, careful not to stumble again.

Liam fell into a long stride, and Rory had to walk fast to keep up. She kept glancing nervously upward at the ceiling. If she stretched out her hand, she was sure she would be able to touch it.

The clopping of mule hooves and the rolling rumble of the steel wheels on the car rails made her look up the tunnel. An instant later, Liam looked at her over his shoulder. "Stay close and pull your cap down."

Rory nodded and adjusted her hat, careful not to touch the hot metal of the lamp this time. The coal car approached, the heavy metal wheels rolling closer. Finally she saw the mule, straining against the tons of coal that it pulled, its head down. As it went past, the driver spat and cursed it, leaning forward to poke at its haunches with a sharp piece of wood.

Two miners passed them a few seconds later, walking the path on the other side of the tracks. They were talking quietly, their picks shouldered. They looked odd, like animals somehow. At first Rory couldn't figure out why, then she realized that they were both tall men, walking with their heads down and their shoulders stooped beneath the tunnel ceiling. She looked up and was startled to see that it had dropped a foot or more.

Rory lifted her free hand and trailed her

fingers along the rock. In the lantern light she could tell that it was the dark slate she had seen all of her life in the culm piles. Tipping her head back, she felt her cap slide and she reached to steady it again.

Liam held out his lantern, gesturing down a dark, narrow tunnel that suddenly gaped on their right. "We were up there a month or so ago. Shorter walk to work."

The parallel iron rails split at the junction of the two tunnels. Rory could see only a dozen or so feet in the light from her lantern. The tunnel might have ended within a hand-span or have gone on forever—there was no way for her to tell.

"Less than a mile to Paddy's door, is all," Liam said.

Rory caught her breath. A mile more. For an instant she imagined the weight of all the rock and coal overhead.

Liam shot her a smile over his shoulder. "We're under Carroll Street now, more or less. We'll go beneath Mill Creek and end up out past Morris Street. We're about a hundred feet lower than the Seven-Foot Vein—it goes even farther."

"It feels strange," Rory told him. "Walking under the town like this."

Liam nodded. "But I don't think about any of that anymore. It's best if you don't."

A scuttling sound caught Rory's attention, and she pulled in a quick breath as two huge rats ran past her feet. Liam seemed not to notice them. His head was turned, looking across the gangway into another branching tunnel.

"That's a good face, down in there. Da said the miners are hauling full coal by noon."

Rory heard the muted scrambling sound again, this time somewhere in a dark space off to their left. "There're a lot of rats down here."

Liam gestured. "The stables are up that way. The rats live on spilled mule feed. You'll see more up by the door. Paddy was feeding two or three to tame them."

"Why?" Rory asked, astonished.

Liam shrugged. "A lot of men do it. The rats are smart. If the air is cut off, they are the first ones to know and they get out."

Rory remembered her father's stories of miners dropping at their work, starved for air. The danger of explosions was worse where the ventilation was bad because the mine gas could accumulate.

Suddenly it seemed to Rory the air in the gangway was heavy. Odd scents of mold and damp made her wrinkle her nose. As they passed a place where the iron rails divided again, she heard rats in the shadows—the quick rustling was almost comforting. She glanced at her lantern. The flame was normal.

A grinding rumble overhead startled Rory, and she ducked instinctively. Liam turned, his eyes scanning the ceiling above them. "It's been working for a few weeks now. Da says it's nothing, just the Seven-Foot Vein settling a little above us."

Rory stood still for a second or two after Liam began walking again. She stared at the ceiling. Were the miners up there staring at the floor?

Liam walked in silence. Rory followed, her nerves raw. The low ceilings were wet, water dripping down the walls. Liam was hunched forward, and Rory kept feeling her cap brush the rock overhead.

Liam stopped at the first door. "I don't know if Jimmy is here yet. But let me show you how it works."

He shouted, and a second later the door was opened from the other side. Rory kept her head down and held her lantern high. She stole a glance at the trapper boy as they went through. He looked very young—maybe nine or ten.

"The mule drivers expect you to hear them coming," Liam told her as they walked on. "You have to stay alert."

Rory nodded.

"By ten o'clock, the cars will be running steady," Liam went on. "They're robbing pillars on this side."

Following him up the shrinking gangway, Rory shivered in the still, damp air. The company had been robbing pillars in the section where Andrew and her father had died. There had been a cave-in, and when the air was cut off, firedamp had exploded.

Rory followed Liam through two more doors. The trappers weren't yet on the job, so he carefully closed the planked gates behind them. Rory noticed a slight uphill grade in the tunnel as they walked.

"Here," Liam said at last.

Rory looked at the door. The wood at the bottom had been chewed into rat-sized notches. The walls were wet with trickling water. She set down her lantern.

"You all right? I'll come back at dinnertime and bring you half of what's in my tin. Tomorrow we'll make sure you have your own dinner."

Rory nodded, turning in a slow circle. The light from her miner's lamp shifted, brushing over the wet, dark stone. There was an overturned apple crate beside the door. Whittled shavings lay thick around it.

"Rory?"

She spun around to face him.

"I'll see you at dinnertime. I don't want to tell Da, so walking you in and out might get to be a problem. But maybe by tomorrow or the next day you can find your own way."

Rory felt a sheen of cold sweat on her forehead. "I don't think I can."

Liam shrugged. "It's easy, Rory. You just stay in the gangway and count the doors and—"

"It isn't easy for me, Liam," she interrupted him.

Liam just looked at her for a few seconds. "Then I'll figure out how to walk you in and out," he promised.

Rory looked at his face, the light from his miner's lamp chiseling it into unfamiliar angles. "I'll be all right," she said. He nodded, then turned and went through the door, swinging his lantern gently at his side. She closed the door behind him, then brought her lantern over to the upturned apple crate and sat down heavily. Liam's footsteps faded.

Rory stared at the darkness beyond the light of her lantern. She could hear only the sound of water dripping. She took a deep breath of the still, damp air, then blew it out again, trying to calm herself. This was only for a few days. Mama would never find out.

An approaching rumble of iron wheels on

the rails made her jump up. The driver shouted, and she leaped to swing the door wide. The mule brushed her shoulder as it went through. The driver never looked at her at all.

Rory watched the coal car for a few seconds, until the shadows swallowed it. The eerie rumbling came again overhead, but ended almost before she had time to get scared. She sat down on her apple crate again and waited, glad the lantern and her lamp held back the darkness.

CHAPTER SEVEN

L iam glanced back toward the door as the coal car passed him. Rory opened it in perfect time, and the car went through. Liam smiled. Rory was nervous, but no worse than most boys would have been. This was going to work out for everyone. Rory would make up her bakery wages, and Mrs. Hamilton would be hovering over Paddy, spooning soup into him and tucking up his blankets.

Liam began to whistle. A short, sharp groaning in the ceiling made him look up. It was working again. If it got bad enough, Kirk and Baum would have a hard time getting the miners to work in this section without raising their pay.

As the gangway narrowed and the ceiling got

lower, coal cars began to pass Liam. The drivers were hauling the day's first empties up into the rooms where the miners would be working. One man was singing an old English song that Mrs. Hamilton sometimes sang in the kitchen. He had a fine voice, and Liam listened, walking a little faster to keep up. When the driver turned off on a siding, Liam was sorry, and he paused to hear the rest of the song. Abruptly, the singing stopped.

Liam just had time to wonder why before a blast of air hit him like a giant fist, shoving him down. His lantern shattered against the rock floor. His miner's lamp was extinguished. In the pitch darkness he heard shouts and curses. Then there was a muted roar somewhere up ahead of him.

"Da!" Liam shouted, scrambling back to his feet. He fumbled with clumsy fingers in his pocket. Finally he managed to fish out the matchbox. He pulled his cap off. Striking a match, he was frightened when the flame flared. He blew it out. He was amazed at his own foolishness. Coal dust was explosive.

Liam stumbled forward in the impenetrable blackness. The gangway was strewn with lumps of coal that had been shattered out of the ribs and ceiling. Blindly, frantically, Liam kept going, his thoughts disjointed.

The air was thick with coal dust. Liam coughed, turning his head to spit gritty saliva. He followed the rails in the dark, kneeling often to feel the cold, solid iron. The rubble increased with every step he took. The menacing rumble in the rock just inches overhead came and went.

Liam clambered up a slanting slab of rock, feeling his way. He scraped his back sliding between the upper edge and the low ceiling, then tumbled downward, falling five or six feet onto a mound of fist-sized coal. He got up slowly, coughing again.

"Is the gangway blocked?"

The shout startled Liam. He turned to face the direction the voice had come from. A second later an iron-strong grip on his jacket spun him around.

"Answer me, ye daft fool!"

Liam tried to tell the man that he didn't know,

but the heavy dust choked him before he could say anything. The miner thumped him on the back until he had recovered.

"Worse or better at the shaft?" the man demanded as Liam straightened up.

"I don't know," Liam croaked, still trying to clear his throat.

"Why are ye headed this way?"

"My Da is up there."

The miner coughed, then spat. "How much farther?"

Liam tried to think clearly. Their room was past the seventh door, Rory was at the fourth. Liam felt a strange sinking stillness inside himself. Rory. He hadn't even thought about her.

"Were ye hit on the head?" This time the miner shook Liam gently, gripping both shoulders.

"No," Liam managed. "Da is beyond the seventh door."

"Gangway's blocked before the sixth, son." The miner coughed, turning Liam around, nudging him back down the passageway.

Liam twisted free, stumbling on the iron

rails. He started to speak, to explain that he had to get to his father, but the choking dust caught at his throat. The miner tried once more, but Liam peeled the man's hands from his shoulders and walked a single step, bumping into the wall. He righted himself and started up the tunnel again, feeling for the rails with his feet.

"Yer daft!" the man shouted after Liam.

Liam heard him but didn't answer. It was hard enough walking blind like this. Without his light, the darkness was complete, terrifying. Sliding both hands along the rib, he made his way slowly forward, placing his feet as well as he could. Where the fallen rock was highest, he climbed slowly, feeling his way.

The miner had been wrong, but not by much. The gangway was blocked just *after* the sixth door. Liam felt the rough planks in the dark, then blundered into a wall of fallen coal only a few paces beyond it. It filled the tunnel top to bottom. Standing on a chunk of coal the size of Mrs. Hamilton's cookstove, Liam banged at the ceiling with one hand, hot tears coursing down his cheeks.

"Da!" he shouted, over and over. The stinging dust coated his mouth and throat and finally stopped his shouts altogether as he doubled over to cough. When he could breathe again, Liam scrambled to the top of the pile and began to dig.

He ran his hands across the fallen rock. The smallest chunks he pitched to one side. Bigger pieces were harder to move, but he managed, bracing his feet and rolling the rocks, clattering and bouncing, down the pile to the floor.

He stopped only when he had to, interrupted by fits of coughing. The air was beginning to clear slightly, but it was still bad, the dust cloying at his nose and mouth. For a time, he thought he was close to breaking through, but the rock seemed endless. He dug at it furiously, making a trough in the pile, but no more than that.

As he worked, Liam's right hand slid across something soft and warm, and he recoiled, startled, then began digging frantically. He pulled away two big slabs of slate, grunting with effort. Then he spread his fingertips and reached downward, grimacing.

His hands slid over the still-warm coat of a mule for a few seconds before he recognized the sharp curve of its hock and the blunt shape of one upturned hoof. Liam sat back on his heels, his heart pounding. There were only a few drivers who came to work this early. Nolan was one of them.

Grimly, Liam set to work again, longing for his miner's lamp. Struggling in the darkness, he followed the shape of the dead mule, clearing a space all the way around it. When he had to, he stood atop the fallen animal, digging with both hands.

The slabs were getting bigger, harder to move. And they were wedged tight, floor to ceiling. He couldn't find the coal car or the driver. He beat at the fallen rock with both hands, then sank to his knees, exhausted, heaving in one painful breath after another.

After Liam's breath quieted, the only sound was the whispery rustle of the rats making their way through the mine. He clasped his hands to pray and felt his fingers stick together. He lifted them, staring into the darkness as though he could see. He made a fist, then loosened it, feeling the odd stickiness again. Blood, he realized finally. He had cut his hands on the rock.

Standing up, Liam felt his way forward, then from side to side, stepping awkwardly over the mule, his boot heel catching in the harness. For an eternal moment, Liam refused to believe it, tugging on one piece of cold stone, then another. All the slabs were big—far too big for him to move, to even budge.

"Da!" Liam shouted at the rockfall, then pressed his ear against one of the slabs. There was no sound, no scraping, no telltale clinking of a pick from the other side. Liam yelled again, then again, pausing to cough, then to listen.

Finally, staggering backward, he fought an urge to throw himself at the rock. It meant nothing that he couldn't hear picks or voices. For all he knew there was a half mile of rock and coal between him and his father.

Liam stood still. The mine was silent around him. The quiet pressed against his ears, making his thoughts seem to shriek inside his skull. What should he do? Rescue parties would come as quick as they could, but how long would that be? Da was probably all right, just waiting for help.

Liam licked his lips, then spit, the bitter taste of coal on his tongue. There was nothing he could do for his father now. He thought about Paddy, lying in his cot at Mrs. Hamilton's. At least he was safe. Liam touched his fingertips together, feeling the sticky wetness of the blood once more. The only thing he could do now was try to get himself out of the mine—and Rory, too. If he could find her.

CHAPTER EIGHT

Rory had been sitting still, listening to the rustling of the rats, when the odd wrenching sound had coursed through the rock over her head. She had jumped up, startled and scared as a strange gust of wind shoved the door wide open. It knocked her down, stinging her eyes with grit and putting out her miner's lamp. Her lantern tipped and rolled, skidding along the rock. Rory saw it flicker and go out as the strange noise faded.

In the darkness that followed, Rory got up, trembling. She heard the rats running, then nothing at all. She fished in her pocket for the box of matches Liam had given her. The darkness in the mine was different from any darkness she had ever experienced. It was so black, so deep and *complete,* like a thousand moonless nights.

Finally, she managed to get the matchbox out of her pocket. Shaking, she opened it and pinched a match between two fingers. She pulled off her cap, then fumbled with the box in the dark, turning it so that the striker was faced upward.

Rory's heart pounded at her rib cage, and her breath was fluttering and quick. The dust was uncomfortably thick, and she cleared her throat, trying not to cough. As she began to drag the match across the striker, she noticed an odd odor in the air. Her hand stopped midmotion as she realized what she was doing.

Her teeth chattering, she shoved the matches back into her pocket, cursing her own stupidity. Coal dust could explode. And the smell might be firedamp—the kind of mine gas that had blown up, killing her father and brother.

"Open the door!"

The voice was shrill. Rory stepped backward, abruptly aware that she was away from the safety of the rib. She could hear the heavy wheels rolling on the tracks, coming toward her. She stumbled on something, half-turning, and realized that she had no idea which way was which. The ink-black darkness was the same in every direction.

"Open the damn door!"

This time she turned toward the voice and moved crosswise, using the shout to orient herself. "It's open," she yelled when she felt the solid wall with her hands. She pressed herself against it, listening to the clopping of mule hooves and the heavy grind of the wheels on the gritty iron rails.

There was a spate of loud coughing, then the voice came again. "How old are you, trapper? You sound like a scared little girl."

Rory clapped one hand over her mouth. Now that something bad had happened, most of the miners would be furious with Liam and Mr. Quinn if she was found out. They could lose their jobs.

"Whoa!" the driver called out. The mule stopped.

"Come on, trapper boy. Come toward my voice." The man cleared his throat again and spat. "Let's get out before anything worse happens."

Rory hesitated, then started forward. She could hear the mule stamping its feet, impatient to get moving. She walked with her hands in front of her, reaching out like a blind person.

"Straight this way." The man's hoarse voice guided her. Rory went slowly, stepping over one rail, afraid the mule might start off without warning. Once or twice a year some unlucky miner lost a hand or leg to the heavy wheels. The thought made her shiver.

"Right here," the driver whispered, and a second later, Rory felt his calloused hand and clasped it. He pulled her forward, and she found herself being lifted. He swung her around and set her on the bumper, her feet dangling downward. She gripped the wood and tried to murmur a thanks, but only coughed in the choking dust.

"Come on, Nightingale," the driver rasped. "Geeup."

The mule leaned into its harness, and Rory listened to the sound of the wheels as they began to roll. It was strange to feel the motion of the car without being able to see the ground moving, or the walls—without knowing what was ahead.

Rory wished the driver would say something—anything to distract her from her thoughts. It was as if he had disappeared. The ink-black darkness had swallowed the mule, the load of coal in the car behind her, everything. For a long time Rory felt as if she were floating through oblivion, that nothing about this glide through the darkness was real. The sound of the wheels grinding over the rails was the only reminder of where she was.

"Head down," the driver warned, and his voice startled her.

Rory bent forward. She almost lost her hold on the bumper, then managed to shift her grip, freeing one hand. She extended her fingertips cautiously and felt the ceiling sliding past less than a foot above her. Had the driver left the gangway? She hadn't walked with

Liam through any tunnel this low, had she?

"Are you lost?" she asked, then coughed as her quick intake of breath pulled the coal dust down into her lungs.

"I trust Nightingale," the miner said.

Her eyes stung and she closed them, listening to the muffled clopping of Nightingale's hooves and the steady metallic grind of the wheels on the rails. She heard the driver curse once under his breath, but he didn't speak and she didn't, either. Her throat ached now.

After a time she felt the coal car tilting slightly. Were they going uphill? The mule was breathing hard. The whole walk with Liam had been *up* a slight incline. She sat very still, afraid to ask, afraid that maybe the mule was just going to get them lost.

The sound of voices made Rory open her eyes. The darkness startled her, even though she had known it was still there. She blinked, narrowing her eyes against the dust. Carefully, she lifted her hand again. The ceiling was even lower here. Rory hitched herself back farther onto the bumper.

"Stay put," the driver ordered hoarsely.

"How far to the shaft?" Rory asked, coughing.

The driver didn't answer. Rory started to ask again, but the angle of the car changed, and she tightened her hands on the bumper. After a full minute crawled past, it leveled out again. The driver cleared his throat and spat.

Rory felt the car change tracks, rolling over the sidings smoothly. The mule was pulling hard now, and she could hear it gasping for a clear breath. Above them was a sound like distant thunder.

The mule stopped, its breath loud and labored. Rory heard the sound of the driver's boots on the ground.

"Nightingale, you have to," he cajoled, his voice rough.

Rory sat very still. If the mule wouldn't go on, they really were lost.

"Pull, Nightingale!" the driver pleaded, and Rory heard the chains jingle as he tugged at the mule's bridle.

Rory could feel coal grit between her teeth. Her eyes ached, and it hurt to breathe. She

listened to the mule cough, a sound like someone retching. She pitied the animal. It'd be
awful to be so out of breath in this stale, dusty
air. "Unhitch the mule."

The driver didn't answer, but the sound of
clinking chains told her that he had already
thought of it. She slid down from the bumper,
bent at the waist, straightening slowly until she
felt the spout on her miner's lamp scrape the
ceiling. Then she hunched forward awkwardly,
waiting.

"Take this," the driver said, finally. Rory
reached out and felt a cool metal chain against
her fingers. Grasping the traces, feeling the links
dig into her palm, Rory waited again, her heart
pounding.

"Geeup," the driver pleaded.

Rory heard the mule shake its head, its bridle jingling. Then there was a tug on the traces
that pulled Rory into a lurching walk. Bent
over to avoid the low ceiling, she stumbled over
a rail tie. Off balance, she misstepped, her heel
striking the rail, then sliding off. She managed
to keep from falling, trying hard not to use the

traces to keep herself upright. If the mule stopped again, it might never go another inch. She walked behind it, willing the clopping of its hooves to go on.

"Smell that?" the driver demanded abruptly.

Startled, Rory wrinkled her nose against the sharp, penetrating stink of coal. "Smell what? The dust?"

"No. It's better air," the driver said.

Rory tried to inhale a little deeper and only made herself cough again.

"Nightingale smells it."

The words, barely audible, lifted Rory's heart. Mules were supposed to be able to smell good air long before a person could. Better air. If it was true, that meant this tunnel led to a ventilated part of the mine. Maybe they could get out.

Without warning, the driver stumbled against Rory, and she fell, sprawling face first onto the ties. Her leg went over one rail, slamming painfully against the metal. She rolled onto her side, hugging her knee, coughing.

Then, panicked, she scrambled to her feet,

banging the top of her head on the ceiling and dropping back into a crouch. Her cap was gone, she realized. She searched the ground with frantic fingertips. She knew she couldn't light it until the dust settled, but the idea of being helpless against the darkness was almost more than she could bear. A sudden tight grip on the back of her jacket made her wrench around.

"Here," the driver's voice came out of the dark. He felt for her wrist, pressing the trace into her hand again.

Rory gripped the chain, tears rising in her eyes. The mule hadn't left them. It had stopped the moment the driver had stumbled. When it started walking again, Rory followed, guided by the traces and the sound of its hooves. The driver stumbled along beside her. Without the weight of the car to pull, the mule went a little faster, and its breathing was less harsh.

It was hard to keep up. The ties were uneven, and Rory had to fight for her footing. It was so dark. She couldn't see her own feet, or the rails, or tell which way the tunnel led. She could hear the wheezing of the driver's breath and smell the sour odor of his sweat. Ahead of them, the mule walked steadily.

Rory's fear rose with every step. At any instant, she knew, an accidental spark somewhere in the mine could ignite the coal dust, turning the tunnels into giant cannon barrels. The blast that had killed her father and brother had rolled six-ton coal cars onto their sides and skidded them down the gangway.

The ceiling got lower, forcing her to bend at the waist as the mule led them along. It seemed to know where it was going, turning twice to the right, taking them through openings that Rory could not see at all. The driver was silent except to spit or cough.

Rory said prayers for Liam and his father, and for any other miner who had been caught by the cave-in. Mama and Paddy would know by now there had been a crush—the mine whistle would have alerted the whole town. Rory was glad her mother didn't know she was in the mine—at least she wouldn't have to worry.

The ground beneath Rory's feet suddenly

smoothed, and she heard the driver make a sound of surprise.

"The stables," he said aloud. "You can stand up."

Rory straightened cautiously. A second later, she bumped into something and reached out to steady herself, feeling the slick-coated shoulder of another mule. It shied away from her, and she nearly lost her balance as Nightingale made a sharp turn, then stopped.

"It's her stall," the driver rasped.

Rory stood, still holding the trace chain, facing the direction the driver's voice had come from. "Where's the shaft?"

The driver said nothing, and Rory felt him take hold of her jacket sleeve. She dropped the trace and let him lead her across the smooth floor. She could hear mules moving in the darkness, and twice the driver slapped at animals in his way.

When Rory stepped back onto railroad ties and rough gravel, she knew they had left the stable. The dark was still impenetrable, directionless. The driver hesitated. Just then, the unmistakable sound of picks striking stone came through the darkness.

"Who's there?" the driver rasped, his voice muted with dust.

There was no answer, but the sound of the picks continued, and the driver began walking. Rory let him lead her along, hoping desperately she would soon see the dull light from the shaft, that the air would be clearer and her breath could come easier.

"Halloo," the driver called.

This time the picking faltered, then stopped, and someone answered, "Over here!"

The driver veered toward the voice, and Rory skinned her knuckles on something in the dark. She flinched and almost cried out, but the dust choked her again and she could only cough.

"Is the shaft cut off?" she heard the driver ask.

The answer was short—two ugly little words: "It is."

CHAPTER NINE

Liam had followed the gangway by trailing one aching hand on the rib every step of the way. Where it opened up into rooms and passages, he walked as straight a line as he could to get by them, bumping one foot along the outer rail to guide himself.

He longed for light and air. The dust thrown up by the rock falls had seeped into his eyes and nostrils and mouth. He could not take a deep breath. His whole body was tense, alert, his heart thudding inside his chest. He forced his thoughts away from Da, trying not to imagine him dead or hurt. There would be help soon. Every miner in St. Claire would be working at the rockfalls.

Liam's already raw fingers stung as he walked,

one hand brushing the wall. If he didn't get mixed up or turned around, it'd take him half an hour or so to get back up to the shaft, walking this slow.

Half an hour. Liam balled his free hand into a fist, ignoring the pain. Half an hour to find help, half an hour back, then whatever time it took to get through the wall of debris. . . . If Da was in trouble, that was too long.

Liam tried to walk faster. The dust clawed at his throat every time he inhaled, and he felt dizzy, disoriented. But he had no way of knowing if that was lack of air and he was about to pass out from black damp, or if he was just shaky from the endless darkness and his own fear.

Liam's right foot struck something. He fought for his balance, his arms flailing as he stepped backward. A fist-sized rock rolled beneath his boot heel and he spun, pitching sideways. Staggering four or five steps, trying not to fall, Liam stumbled over a rail and finally went down, sprawling onto his belly.

He turned onto his back, wincing. He lay very still, blinking, looking straight up into the blackness. Why hadn't he bumped into the wall? He had taken five or six steps, hadn't he? The only logical answer was that he had happened to trip near an opening in the wall.

Many of the coal rooms were big, many of them were connected by short, rough tunnels. Liam tried to relive the fall, to understand the motions his body had gone through. He didn't want to get confused and wander into a maze of unworked rooms away from the gangway where rescuers might miss him when they came.

Without moving, Liam wiped at his face with his sleeve, fighting panic. Had he fallen forward? He remembered turning on his heel, trying not to fall. Had he turned all the way around? He reached out one hand, feeling for the rails. The cool metal was close to him, closer than he had thought. He sat up.

Maybe he was still in the gangway, then. Maybe he hadn't stumbled through a passage. He stood up and took two steps, relieved, coughing a little, adjusting his cap. Then he hesitated. He squatted to feel the rail and caught his breath, running his hand along it as far as he could reach. It was curved.

Liam tried to think clearly. The rails curved where a track left the main line. So he had gone through an opening in the wall. But which way was the gangway? He took three more steps, then stooped to feel the rail again. It was straightening out. Turning around, he walked carefully, sliding one foot along the rail as he followed it back.

Bending over the curving rail, he slid his fingers along the metal, finally coming to the place where the track split. The switch was open so that coal cars coming down the gangway toward the shaft would go straight past. Liam stood and walked three careful paces down the track, then stepped sideways until he felt the solid wall beneath his right hand again.

His heart still pounding, Liam kept going, one step after another. The dark was like a heavy hand, weighing on him. He suddenly coughed so hard that he had to stop, doubling over, gasping for breath. As he straightened, he heard voices.

For an instant the voices sounded ghostly, and he imagined a procession of long-dead miners walking the gangways like they did in Da's stories. The voices faded, then started again. Liam tried hard to make out what the men were saying. He couldn't. As he crossed an opening, his right arm outstretched to find the wall where it picked up on the far side, the voices got louder. He stopped.

"All right in there?" he called, then choked, unable to hear an answer if there was one. He called out again once he had stopped coughing. This time, he heard a shout in response. It filled him with an unreasoning joy.

"I'm here!" he called, triggering another coughing fit. The answer seemed louder, closer. He shouted again, as loudly as he could before the dust caught at his throat and gagged him.

"Is that the shaft gangway?" The voice was louder now, clearer.

"Yes," Liam shouted as best he could, "I think so."

"Keep talking!"

Liam tried. Every twenty or thirty seconds

he called out again, then coughed up the coal dust he had inhaled. He heard the footsteps and the rasping whispers of the men as they came toward him.

"We're timber setters," a man said.

"Thompson's hurt," a different voice added.

Liam stared. The men were probably less than three feet away and yet they were invisible, along with everything else. He knew they were the men he had joked with earlier, but he couldn't recall any of their faces, or even how many of them there were.

"It's blocked off up above," Liam told them, pushing the words past the infuriating tickle and sting of the dust. "The shaft might be clear." He hoped it was true. If it was, Rory should be out and safe by now—and help was on its way.

"If it's not open, there're the connectors that run up to the Seven-Foot Vein," the first man said.

"We'll never get Thompson up that," one of the others put in. "Not with this leg."

Liam stood, listening. He hadn't thought of

the connecting tunnels. Kirk and Baum had commissioned several to increase the ventilation back when they were digging the new shaft on the Seven-Foot Vein. He wasn't sure where they came in to the Mammoth, and in this dark, he was positive he'd never find any of them.

"Thompson's bleeding bad, Mick," a voice interrupted Liam's thoughts.

"How many are you?" Liam asked, getting an idea.

"Five," one of the men said. "But Thompson—"

"Can two of you help me dig through to my Da?" Liam interrupted.

"How far back in?" one of the men asked.

Liam stared at the darkness in the direction of the voice. "Half a mile."

"The shaft is closer," another man said. "And we don't have tools."

"We can find picks," Liam began, then coughed, knowing that what he was asking them to do was unreasonable—maybe even impossible.

For a few seconds there was only the sound

of men coughing, then someone else spoke. "Your pa could already be out."

There was a general murmur of agreement.

"There're the braitch holes up there, Mick," someone said.

"Let's make the shaft first."

Liam had no idea which of them had said it, but they all made sounds of assent. They were right, and he knew it. There was no reason to think they could find tools, then get through the fall—especially with the air this bad.

Heavyhearted, Liam started walking. After a few seconds, he heard the men behind him. It was odd to listen to their footsteps and know that they were so close—and that if he turned, he wouldn't be able to see any of them.

Still, the sound of footsteps was comforting. The black, endless gangway was less frightening now that he wasn't alone. Liam heard a groan of pain behind him, and slowed. Thompson was obviously hurt pretty bad. Liam hoped the shaft was open. Maybe there were already rescuers coming down into the mine carrying picks and shovels and stretchers for the wounded.

The gangway was easy enough to follow so long as Liam trailed one hand on the rib. Here, closer to the shaft, the rockfall had been much less. They crossed a few places where rubble littered the floor, but nowhere did they have to climb rocks the way he'd had to further in.

Liam said a prayer for his father, then another for Rory, using the rhythm of the words to time his steps. The shaft couldn't be too far now.

Liam's right hand left the rib and was suddenly trailing through empty air. He kept walking, trying to take a fairly straight line, but it scared him to be without the guidance of the solid wall.

What sounded like a muffled shout in the rooms off to his right made him stop. The men behind him had heard it as well and paused, too. Liam listened hard, trying to still the racket of his own harsh breathing. After a moment, the sound came again, and he felt a cold weight of fear settle on his shoulders as it swelled, roaring through the rock overhead. It was no human voice. It was the sound of the tortured rock moving again.

CHAPTER TEN

Rory was off to one side, moving rock back from where the men were working. She had been careful not to talk much and to keep her voice low. The dust was awful, and the men were coughing almost constantly. Rory's throat was raw and stinging.

"Who's there?" one of the miners shouted suddenly.

"Timber setters," a voice called back. "Five of us." The man coughed, then went on. "We've got one man hurt, and there's a lad on his own."

The sound of picks stopped as the miners listened.

"How far up is the gangway open?" one of the miners asked as the footsteps came closer.

"There's a fall at the sixth door. My Da's on the other side of it."

Rory recognized Liam's voice. She started to call out, then caught herself. She took a step forward and waited as the men came closer. She listened to them talking, deciding where to settle the injured man, where to begin helping to clear the shaft. She made her way closer, carefully tracking Liam by his voice. When the men told him where to start carrying rock, she followed him cautiously.

Two of the men began to argue. One of the timber setters was afraid of sparks being struck by the picks. The others thought it was worth the risk. Rory heard Liam begin lifting rock. As he walked away from the others, she moved closer.

"Liam?" she said quietly. There was a sharp grinding sound, coal chips beneath a boot.

"Rory?"

"Yes." She felt tears flood her eyes and clasped her hands together to keep them from shaking. "What should we do?"

Liam was silent for a long moment. "I'd hoped the shaft would be open."

Rory leaned closer so she could whisper. "They couldn't hear picks on the other side."

"It's a big fall." Liam's answer was almost too quiet to hear, and Rory found herself glancing toward the darkness where the miners were working.

A sudden, rending crack made Rory jerk around, scanning the blackness. She felt Liam put his hand on her shoulder as the collapsing rock began to crash around them.

There was a scream of pain, somewhere off to Rory's left. Something struck the side of her face, and she cried out. Liam grabbed a handful of her jacket sleeve and dragged her forward. She stumbled, and Liam jerked her back onto her feet, shouting something she couldn't understand.

Behind them, the rock fell like thunder. Terrified, Rory ran, Liam still gripping her hand. Chunks of slate and coal rolled beneath her feet and she skidded, blundering into Liam. Their feet tangled, but somehow, miraculously, they managed to keep going, fleeing blindly up the gangway.

Rory could hear men screaming over the pounding of her own footsteps and the rattling slide of the crush. There were no thoughts in her mind, only pure fear. She ran over the uneven railroad ties and piles of rock faster than she had ever run before.

Bent forward, running all out, Rory hooked her foot on a rail. She slammed sideways into the wall, pulling Liam with her. She fell, hitting so hard that for a few seconds she couldn't draw in a breath—and when she did, it only made her convulse, coughing.

Somewhere beside her she heard Liam groaning and realized that the deafening rumble of the rockfall had stopped. There was a strange numbness in her right arm and a sharp pain above her eye. She could hear Liam moving in the darkness.

The choking dust had thickened. Rory covered her mouth with her arm, breathing through the cloth of Paddy's jacket. She listened, her heart pounding. There were no screams now, no voices at all. Liam was struggling to sit up, and she shifted to one side to give him room. Propped against the wall they had crashed into, Rory coughed, trying to free her voice to ask if he was hurt.

Liam managed to speak first, in a low, rough whisper. "Are you all right?"

She nodded. "I think so."

She could hear him gagging. Then he cleared his throat and shouted hoarsely, "Is anyone there?"

There was no answer, and Rory found herself crying again.

"Can anyone hear me?" Liam called out again.

There was no response from the silent darkness. Rory listened as he called again, then again. No answer.

Rory's tears seemed too hot against her cheeks, and her forehead ached. The choking dust was more than she could bear. Liam was still shouting. She prayed for someone to answer him, but no one did.

"We can't stay here," Liam said finally, his voice ragged. "We'll suffocate."

Rory turned toward him, hating the dark, terrified to move, but more scared to stay. She coughed, a painful, racking spasm. She wanted to be home. She wanted her mother. If she got out alive, she would never complain about her chores again. She could feel Liam's hand on her shoulder as he steadied himself to stand up.

She got to her feet and clasped his hand. He set off slowly, and the uneven cadence of his walk told her he was limping. She kept up, walking with her free hand extended forward, protecting her face. Her shoulder still ached, but the odd numbness was receding.

In the silence that had followed the roar of the rockfall, Rory could hear Liam shuffling his feet through the chunks of rock and coal.

"Stay between the rails," he whispered.

Rory slid one foot forward cautiously and bent over to feel the rail to her left, then turned to touch the one on the right. Liam walked slowly, and she followed.

She tried to think about placing her feet carefully, about taking shallow breaths to keep from coughing. She shoved back her other thoughts, the ones that circled her in the dark.

★   ★   ★

Liam's leg hurt. It was all he could do to keep walking. Every two or three steps he felt the side of his boot bump the rail and he corrected his path slightly. Maybe this was crazy. But how could it be more dangerous than staying in a place where the ceiling was falling in?

"Wait," Rory said from behind him. He stopped. He could hear a little scuffling sound. Rats were in the gangway now.

"My shoe's come undone," Rory said, then coughed.

He waited until she stood up, wishing they could talk without choking on the coal dust. She had to be thinking about her father and brother, and she had to be scared half to death. It was awful to be in the dark like this, even for him, and he knew the mine pretty well.

"Ready," Rory whispered, standing up.

Liam took her hand awkwardly in the dark, touching her shoulder first, then running his hand down her sleeve. She gripped his fingers tightly, and he could feel her trembling as they started off.

Liam kept his free hand moving, sweeping a

wide arc in front of him. He had no intention of running into anything else. Rory held tightly to his hand. Liam kept clearing his throat, fighting to breathe, trying not to think about his father.

Liam hoped they could find someplace where the air was a little better. Then, maybe they could hold out until help came. He knew there were braitch holes farther up in the mine, but he was pretty sure none of the man-sized vertical ventilation holes had been drilled this close to the shaft.

Sometimes on Sundays, he and Nolan came upon the open holes in the woods and dropped pebbles down, lying on their bellies to hear them hit. Some of the braitch hole ladders were old and rotting, but he knew he would chance it right now if there was one he could get to.

Liam wondered again if he was leading Rory into more danger, or less. He was glad she was with him, he admitted to himself as he slowed to pick his way through more fallen rock. He did not want to be alone. It was lucky that so few had been in the mine when the cave-in happened, but it was eerie, too. The silent gangways were too much like graves.

Liam shook his head to get rid of the thought.

"What?" Rory asked. "Is something wrong?"

He shrugged. "Nothing." He chided himself for almost letting her know how scared he was. It would only frighten her more if she knew.

"It's harder to breathe," Rory rasped.

Liam started to explain that the dust would thin as they got farther from the last cave-in— then he hesitated. It might not be true if there had been another cave-in up ahead. Besides, it wasn't just the dust, and he didn't want to tell her that.

Walking carefully, Liam tried to think it through. The shaft acted as the downcast. The furnace atop the new slope drew stale air out of the other side of the colliery—pulling fresh air in here. Blocked tunnels meant blocked air. And it was more than a matter of having fresh air to breathe. Firedamp built up in stagnant air. Sometimes black damp, too, which was just as dangerous.

Miners sometimes didn't know the bad air

was making them sick until they lost feeling in their legs and fell down. If no one found them in time, they could die. Liam pulled in a deep breath without meaning to and immediately began to cough.

"I have a headache," Rory said, and Liam held her hand tighter. A headache was another sign of bad air.

Liam had been so concerned about his father that he hadn't shown much sense. He should have been figuring out while his head was clear where the air would last the longest. If he waited much longer, his thoughts would get muddled and he wouldn't be able to think at all.

Forcing himself to focus, Liam tried to think of every possible air source. The list was short, and he could tick off almost every item on it. The shaft was blocked. The only gangway that led toward the best ventilated part of the mine had caved in. They were cut off from the braitch holes. That only left the new connecting tunnels. And he had no idea how to find one. Liam felt like a fool. The timber setters had known, and he hadn't asked.

"Isn't there a way out, Liam?" Rory's voice was so harsh, he could barely understand her.

"Air will be better up ahead," he lied. There was no reason for the air to get anything but worse. He could only hope that Da had better luck. Maybe, Liam thought, his father was just fine on the other side of the mound of coal and rock, and was worrying about *him*.

Liam felt Rory trip over something and he tightened his grip on her hand as she righted herself. She lapsed into a long fit of coughing, and he slowed to let her bend forward at the waist. How would he ever explain to her mother if he got out and she didn't? How would he ever explain it to himself?

Liam felt helpless, desperate. What could he do? The coal mine was like a maze. Even if he knew where a connector tunnel was, he could walk right past it in this damnable dark.

Liam imagined Paddy lying on his cot. What would happen to him and the girls if he and Da died today? Aunt Mary couldn't possibly afford to take care of them. Liam squared his shoulders, clearing his throat. The dust was a little thinner here. Maybe he could find some part of the mine where they could wait it out.

"Liam!" He paused when Rory tugged at his hand. "Hear that?"

He tilted his head, listening. There was nothing but the complete stillness that had settled over the gangway after the last cave-in.

"I don't hear—" he began, then stopped. A sound like a distant birdsong was coming from somewhere up ahead of them.

Liam started forward, pulling Rory along with him.

"Wait," Rory said, and jerked her hand free of his. She stopped. "It's to your left somewhere."

Just then, the reedy whistle began again. Liam held still, listening. She was right.

Liam tried to think clearly. If they left the gangway to follow the sound, he wasn't at all sure they could find their way back. The rooms in this section were odd sizes. The walls angled differently; every miner had his own way of doing things.

Liam squeezed Rory's hand, knowing she

wasn't going to like what he was about to say, but it was the only solution. "Wait here."

Rory clutched his hand. "No, I'll go, too."

"No, you can't," Liam said. "We'll get lost. You can yell and guide me back."

He felt her hand loosen on his and he could imagine the expression on her face. He didn't blame her. The thought of being alone scared him, too. But separating was the only way to make sure they didn't lose the gangway. When help came, he didn't want to be half unconscious at the back of some unworked room where no one would look for days.

"Wait by the wall," he said, guiding her sideways, making sure she had found the rib. "Rory," he began, then he had to stop to clear his throat. She let go of his hand, and when he could speak again, it was strange, knowing she was there but unable to see her at all. "Stay right here."

"I will." Her voice was small and frightened.

"I'll hurry," Liam promised. Then he turned away from her, walking toward the weak, whistling sound.

CHAPTER ELEVEN

Liam stepped over the rail and moved away from Rory slowly, fighting an irrational urge to glance back. He knew there was no point; it was impossible to see anything. The utter lack of light seemed to press at his forehead and eyes, like a blindfold tied tightly around his head.

Liam's outstretched fingers touched the rib, the rough rock wall grating at his already raw skin. He stopped and turned toward the whistling, feeling his way toward the opening he knew had to be there.

Liam slid his feet along, determined not to stumble and fall again, pushing aside the coal and rock fragments as he went. When he came to the passage, he paused and listened. The whistle was louder here. He turned back. "Can you hear me, Rory?"

"Yes," she answered instantly.

"Stay right there."

"I will," she said, and then began to cough.

Reassured, Liam eased his way through the opening, both hands up, protecting his face. The whistling had softened, and he wondered if he had made a mistake. Maybe it was coming from someplace farther away than he had thought. He veered slightly to his left, wishing he knew the layout of these rooms.

The Mammoth Vein had both small and massive pillars. His fingers brushed a solid wall, and he took two steps to the right, following it. As abruptly as it had begun, it ended. Small pillars here, then, he thought. So they would be close together.

Liam's left foot bumped a rail, and he allowed it to guide his direction. The tracks would end near the face of coal that was being worked. The whistling stopped suddenly, and Liam paused midstep.

"Is someone there?" a strained, husky voice called out, followed by the sound of choking.

"It's Liam Quinn, Gerrick Quinn's son," Liam answered.

"Liam?" came the crack-voiced response, and Liam recognized Nolan's thick County Cork accent.

"Where are you, Nolan?" Liam found himself smiling, overjoyed.

"Here!"

Liam turned. "Keep talking."

"This way, Liam," Nolan yelled hoarsely.

Liam walked faster, hope and fear soaring inside him now. Nolan sounded all right, but something was wrong or he wouldn't be whistling for help. He knew the mine as well as anyone—the drivers all did. He wasn't just lost.

"Nolan?"

"You're close, Liam, keep coming."

Liam stepped carefully, following the sound of Nolan's voice. As he got closer, he could tell that Nolan was sitting down, or lying down; his voice was coming from near the floor.

"Are you all right?" he whispered, kneeling

to sweep the air with his hands until he touched Nolan's shoulder.

"Lucky's hurt bad," Nolan said sadly.

For the first time, Liam noticed the shallow, labored breathing of the mule. Nolan took Liam's hand and placed it on the animal's neck. "She knows you, Liam. She's glad you're here."

Liam stroked the mule's slick coat, searching for words of sympathy for Nolan. He loved the mule like it was family, Liam knew. A distant creaking rolled through the rock overhead, and Liam felt the mule tense, lifting her head.

"Easy, Lucky," Nolan murmured.

Liam sat back on his heels. "Do you know a way out, Nolan?" He cleared his throat, feeling grit between his teeth.

"I'm staying, Liam." Nolan's voice was strained.

"You can't," Liam argued, a sick feeling in the pit of his stomach.

"I won't leave Lucky." Nolan's voice was flat, choked.

Liam reached out to grip his shoulder. "Lucky's a good mule, Nolan," Liam began, then had to cough. "But you can't help her," he added when he had gotten his breath again.

"I won't leave her alone," Nolan insisted, his voice brittle.

"You have to," Liam said. "The gangway is blocked at the sixth door and by the shaft. Some have been killed, Nolan."

"Paddy?"

Liam didn't know what to say. He didn't have breath or time to explain. "Paddy's fine."

"Your father?" Nolan said in a low voice.

"I don't know," Liam told him. He searched desperately for something to say—something that would make Nolan change his mind. "There's a connector somewhere," he began, meaning to lie about being able to find it. But Nolan cleared his throat and dug his fingers into Liam's forearm to interrupt him.

"It's up four rooms," Nolan said, breathing so deliberately that each word was cut off from the others, a separate effort.

Liam leaned forward. "It is?"

"Halfway up the last face," Nolan managed to say. Then his coughing took over. Each heavy breath seemed to be enormously hard for

Nolan to draw. When his cough subsided, he made an odd sound, a low-pitched groan.

Lowering his hands from Nolan's shoulders, Liam touched hard, jagged stone, and his heart sank. Nolan was half buried.

Once the sound of Liam's footsteps had faded, Rory stood silently. At first, she had waited impatiently. The dark seemed like a solid mass around her, heavy and menacing.

It was so hard to breathe. She could hear Liam coughing and listened intently. How long would it be before he came back? She hugged herself, digging her fingernails into her forearms. There were men back in there, lost or maybe hurt.

Just as she thought it, she could hear Liam's voice again, then someone else's. She held still, straining to make out what they were saying, but she couldn't. All at once, the darkness made her dizzy and she swayed on her feet, fighting an impulse to cry out to Liam to come back.

A quick, scrabbling noise close by startled her. She jumped sideways, sitting down hard. The scuffling sound stopped instantly, then began again. Rats, she thought. They were trapped, too.

Rory touched the cool iron of the rail. She wondered what had happened to the mules in the stable, and tears stung at her eyes. The poor animals had nothing to say about any of this, and she knew they hated the mine. The spring before, when the St. Claire had shut down for a month, the mules had been brought up and put out to pasture. They had all balked at being loaded into the cages and lowered down into the shaft again. Two or three of them had fought so hard that four or five men had ended up beating them into obedience.

Something brushed Rory's hand, and she jerked it away, crossing both arms over her chest. In that instant, the rat clawed its way up the back of her jacket. Rory swiped at it awkwardly, reaching over her own shoulder. The rat clung to the cloth as though its feet were barbed.

Rory pulled at her collar, trying to make the rat jump off. It scrambled for better footing, making a high, growling sound. Frantic, Rory stood, leaning against the wall, pinning the rat.

She wriggled, trying to grind it against the hard rock, to crush it.

A sudden sharp pain just below her shoulder blade made her jackknife. The rat ran to her shoulder. For a long second she could feel its warm fur against her neck. Then she grabbed it and flung it, a grimace of revulsion pulling at her mouth when she heard it hit the wall.

She stood rigidly for a few seconds, then picked up a piece of coal and threw it as hard as she could into the darkness. The sound of the rats scrambling over the rock-strewn ground came from every direction. Had they been in a circle around her?

Rory swallowed nervously. Liam's voice drifted back to her. He was talking fast and low. She heard him coughing, then the second voice again.

"Liam?" she called weakly, then was instantly ashamed of herself. Whoever he was helping was probably in far more trouble than she was. She picked up another chunk of coal and threw it hard, stumbling to one side. She kicked at the ground, scattering shards of rock, then scooped up a handful of coal chips and peppered the ground around herself, turning in a half circle. The sound of the rats running in the darkness seemed endless. How many of them were there?

Rory stooped to pick up more rocks. Her hand touched coal grit, then the cool iron of the rail, then fur. The rat whirled beneath her fingers. Rory felt its long, hairless tail whip across her arm as it fled. Rory gasped, then choked, bending double to cough again.

Rory grabbed up more rocks, inching backward, her right hand cocked to the side, ready to throw. The skittering sounds seemed to be everywhere.

Rory backed into the wall and stood there, her eyes scanning helplessly, the rats invisible in the darkness. She couldn't tell how close they were. She hurled her handful of rocks and heard the rats move backward. Then they drew closer again. She stooped, searching blindly for more rocks.

"Don't, Liam," Nolan kept saying.

Liam ignored him, pulling handfuls of loose rock away from Nolan's back. If all the rock was as small as what was on the surface, he'd be able to dig him out.

"Stop it, Liam," Nolan said more sharply, then leaned forward again to murmur comfortingly into Lucky's long ears.

"I'm going to get you out of here, Nolan." Liam swept away layers of the small stones, then cursed silently. Of course it couldn't be that easy. He rolled back a larger rock, then another from beneath it. He couldn't quit coughing, but he worked steadily. Beneath the two bigger rocks, he found a third, almost too heavy to lift.

"Liam!" Nolan gasped.

Liam stopped. "Did I hurt you?"

Nolan moaned. It was a sound so full of anguish that Liam winced. He made his way around Nolan's side, patting the mule, careful not to startle her. "We have to get you out of here, Nolan."

"No," Nolan said. Then he paused for a few seconds, and Liam could hear him trying not to cough.

"Maybe I can—"

"No, Liam." Nolan's breathing was louder than the mule's now. Liam heard Lucky lift her head, then Nolan's soothing voice as he calmed her down.

For a long moment, Liam sat still, fighting indecision. If the rock was somehow supporting Nolan, maybe he should leave it alone until there was more help to carry him quickly out into the fresh air. But what if there was another cave-in, or an explosion? What if help didn't come and Nolan suffocated right here? Leaving him might be the same as abandoning him to death.

"I won't leave Lucky," Nolan said as if he had heard Liam's thoughts. Nolan's halting speech was ended in a coughing fit.

Liam put his arm around Nolan's shoulders, dangerously close to crying. What should he do? What *could* he do? He couldn't even save himself.

"I'll get you out," he said, starting to stand up.

Nolan grabbed his sleeve. "No."

Liam shook his head fiercely, wishing he could see Nolan's face. "I can't just leave you. What if—"

"I can't feel anything in my legs, Liam. I can't walk."

Liam reeled backward, cold shock settling in his stomach. He couldn't possibly carry Nolan without a stretcher, not even with Rory's help. But how could he walk away?

"When help comes through, you can tell them where we are," Nolan whispered. "Tell my ma I love her."

Fighting tears, Liam nodded, then remembered that Nolan couldn't see him. "I will," he promised.

Nolan said no more, and Liam thought he was coughing again, then realized that he was crying. "Go on, Liam," he managed after a moment. "Please."

Liam stood, reaching back down to clasp Nolan's shoulder for an instant. There was nothing more to say or do, but it still took him a moment to take the first step away, then the second. He walked on, directionless, until he couldn't stand it anymore. Then he shouted to Rory.

When she didn't answer for a few seconds, it scared him.

"Liam?" she shouted, finally. Her voice was full of panic, and a second later, she screamed. Liam started toward her, going as fast as he dared.

CHAPTER TWELVE

Rory covered her mouth with both hands to keep from screaming again. The rats were running up her legs, clinging to the thick cloth of her borrowed trousers.

She knocked three of them away, skinning her knuckles on the rough wall. She could feel a trickle of blood on her skin. There was a rush of tiny, almost inaudible clicking of rats' claws on the hard stone. Were they coming toward her? Could they smell the blood?

"Rory?"

"Liam!" she tried to shout, but her throat was too raw, too thick with dust.

"Rory? Where are you?"

"Here!" she answered, almost dizzy with relief.

A moment later he was beside her, listening to her cracked and painful voice as she explained about the rats. Leaning close to her ear, whispering, he told her about his friend Nolan. She knew Nolan a little. He was always quiet and polite when he came into the bakery.

"Will he be all right, Liam?" she asked.

"I don't think so." Liam's voice was hollow.

Rory squeezed her eyes shut, trying to focus her thoughts. She could still hear the rats moving on the stone. "What are we going to do?"

Liam leaned close again, and she realized that his voice was about gone. "There's a ventilation tunnel that connects to the Seven-Foot Vein," he whispered. "Nolan told me where." He coughed, then reached for her hand, nudging her into a slow, cautious walk.

Rory's thoughts were an odd whirl. Where had the rats gone? She couldn't hear them now. She took little steps, mincing along, afraid to walk any faster. Liam didn't seem to mind. She heard him counting as they passed gaps in the wall.

As she let Liam lead her along, the air felt thick as soup in her lungs, and Rory could feel her headache getting worse. It throbbed now, deep inside her skull, and she knew it had something to do with the bad air. Her father had talked endlessly about firedamp and black damp and a poison air called whitedamp. She wished desperately that she had asked him more questions, that she had learned more about the dangers underground.

Rory wanted to ask Liam about the air, but it seemed too hard to form the words. She was so tired. The rats had frightened her almost out of her wits. She kicked a spray of rock out to the side and heard startled squeaks amid the faint rattle as the pebbles settled into the coal dust. Were the rats running along beside them now? Why would they?

"Rory," Liam said. "This way." He tugged at her hand.

Rory followed him as he turned. This was the fourth room, then. She tried to recall what else Liam had told her, but she couldn't. "I feel sick."

"The air is blocked," Liam said.

Rory heard him, but his words seemed distant, hard to understand. She followed him, hearing the rats again. When Liam stopped, she waited while he moved along the face of coal, patting at it, feeling for the opening.

"Here it is," he said finally.

Rory felt her heart lift a little. If she could just move her heavy legs, get herself up the tunnel, maybe she would be safe after all.

"It's narrow," Liam rasped, then spat. "We'll have to crawl."

Rory walked toward the sound of his voice. She slid her hands along the rough opening in the rock.

"In here, Rory."

She felt the end of the wall and stood still, hesitating beside the opening. Liam was already inside.

"Rory?"

She took a cautious step, her arms out. She could hear him moving away from her, making room, little pebbles rolling beneath his boots.

"Wait for me," she said uneasily, taking another step.

"I'm right here," Liam said. He took in a quick breath, and Rory hesitated.

"What's wrong?"

He cleared his throat. "This is where the rats are going, Rory."

The instant he said it, she realized she had been hearing them all along. She knew she should be glad. It meant they thought this was the way out, too. She touched the rock, gauging the height of the tunnel. Then she ducked her head and dropped to all fours to crawl inside. She hadn't gone more than a few feet when a rat scrambled across her hand. Startled, she slapped at it.

"Don't," Liam said. "They'll bite."

Rory blinked.

"Just ignore them," Liam said.

"I can't," she whispered quietly enough that he couldn't hear her as he turned and started up the tunnel.

The tunnel was narrow. The rats were like a living current on either side of them. Rory crawled, easing her hands onto the stone, carefully transferring her weight from one knee to the other. She was afraid of pinching a paw or a tail and being bitten again.

The rock was rough, pitted with pick marks and the shatter scars of blasting. It ground at Rory's knees as she crawled. She wondered dully about Liam's leg and tried to remember if he had been limping back in the gangway. She couldn't.

"It gets smaller again up here," Liam said over his shoulder.

Rory nodded but bumped her head, anyway, not expecting the tunnel ceiling to drop as low as it did. The rock was cool and sharp, and she blinked back tears at the sudden pain. Then she ducked and kept her chin almost on her chest as she went on.

Once they were up in the Seven-Foot Vein, she would be able to get away from the stale smell of the rats, to rest. She clung to that hope. Sliding her hands along the stone, nudging rats out of the way, she said a prayer for Nolan and another for Liam's Da. As she finished, it struck her that her thoughts were no longer quite as confused as they had been. She pulled in a deep breath and was surprised not to cough.

As they went, the tunnel slanted gradually upward. Rory heard a sudden squeal, and Liam cursed. A ripple ran through the current of rats. Rory lifted her head sharply, wishing desperately that she could stand up and walk instead of crawl. It made her uneasy to have the rats so close to her face. She kept imagining them suddenly turning to attack her, their long, yellowed teeth gnawing at her.

Rory shuddered and closed her eyes, pressing her lips together to keep from crying out. She counted slowly to fifty as she crawled, then started over, recoiling every time she felt fur slide across her skin.

Liam stopped abruptly, and Rory blundered into him, then lurched to the side, trying not to fall. Rats scrambled to get out of the way, crawling over her legs. Shoving herself upright, she sat back on her heels, startled at how low the ceiling was now. She skinned her shoulder blades against the rough rock, then held still for a moment, crouching, her body wedged between the floor and the ceiling.

"Are you all right?" Liam asked.

"I think so," Rory answered. She knew she needed to get going, to crawl again. But she was jammed into the tunnel like a cork in a bottle. Her back was arched against the stone ceiling, and when she put out one hand to steady herself she felt the tunnel wall only a few inches from her side. Her feet were trapped beneath her. She fought to keep from falling backward; the tunnel sloped away behind her.

Rory felt sweat trickle down her temple. The rats were wriggling past, squirming between her and rock. She leaned forward, slowly working one foot free, then the other. Rats skittered out of the way. Placing the palms of her hands on the bottom of the tunnel again was difficult. Every time she reached out, she touched rat fur.

"Are you ready?" Liam asked.

"I hate them," Rory whispered. Tears were welling up in her eyes, but she didn't feel like crying; she felt like screaming. "How much farther?" she asked.

"I don't know." Liam's voice was tight and uneasy.

Rory tried once more to find bare rock with

her right hand. This time, she gritted her teeth and forced herself to lower her hand gradually, letting the rats run beneath her palm.

"Should I go on?" There was an edge of panic in Liam's voice, but Rory ignored him. Her left hand was close to the rats' backs. She hesitated, then lowered it another inch, supporting herself with her right hand. She felt whiskers prickle against her skin and bit her lip to keep from snatching her hand away.

A second later, she shifted her weight to her left hand, lifting her right again as she slid one knee forward. She bumped into Liam's boots. "Go on," she pleaded, knowing that if she stopped she might never be able to force herself to move again.

Liam said something as he began to crawl, his voice low and tense. She couldn't understand him, but it didn't matter. The only thing that she cared about was getting to the end of the tunnel and away from the rats.

The slope steepened a little. The rats ran faster, zigzagging across her legs. They were frantic now, squealing and biting at each other. Rory's heart was slamming at her ribs. The rats were everywhere. She could hear them and feel them and, for the first time, she was almost grateful for darkness that kept her from being able to see them.

Without warning, Liam stopped, and Rory ran into him. He cried out, and for a moment she thought she had somehow hurt him.

She tugged at his ankle. "What? Are you all right?"

Liam answered with a pain-filled cry that unnerved her so much that it took half a minute for her to understand what he was saying over and over.

"It's closed off," he whispered. "The tunnel is blocked, Rory."

She lunged forward, her hand extended, her fingertips stiff. Her weight flattened him against one side of the passage. As she fell, pinning rats beneath her body, she felt what she dreaded and feared more than anything. Rory slid backward again, curling up, cradling the fear that ached inside her. Rats poured over her as she rocked back and forth, terrified. They were trapped. Oh dear God, they were trapped.

CHAPTER THIRTEEN

Rory closed her eyes against the darkness and screamed. They were going to die in the mine. She was never going to see her mother again. Rats were scrambling over her. Liam was shouting—Rory could hear his voice through the ringing curtain of her own—but she still could not stop screaming.

"Rory!"

Liam was shaking her now, shouting her name. Rory felt her scream shrinking, folding itself up until all that was left was a whimper that convulsed her stomach and made her feel small and weak.

He let go of her shoulders. "Rory!"

She managed to draw in a long, shuddering breath. "I'm sorry."

"There's a hole somewhere," he said. "The rats are making it out. We'll be safer here."

"Safer?" Rory repeated. It still hurt to breathe, but the choking dust had not risen this far. And her light-headedness had gone. Liam must be right. The air was better.

"I think we can roll some of this rock out of our way," Liam said over his shoulder. "Maybe we can get through."

Rory pulled in an uneven breath, her whole body still shaking. She could hear rock sliding against rock, a grating sound. A few seconds later, Liam pushed a stone the size of a winter cabbage into her leg. She picked it up and lifted it over her lap, then shoved it downhill. She could hear it rolling and the startled squeals of the rats.

"Here," Liam said.

Slowly, giving the rats time to get out of the way, Rory dragged a bigger piece of rock toward herself. She managed to kneel, then swing it back and forth, releasing it so that it bounced down the slanting tunnel. She heard rats squeal again.

"This one's heavier," Liam said. She could hear him dragging a rock along the floor. "Can you manage it?"

Rory squatted, reaching out in the blackness. The rock was flatter and harder to move. But she upended it, then crouched, backing down the tunnel a little ways, dragging it along. Rats streamed around her feet and ankles.

When it would not roll, Rory finally left it, but a new thought was troubling her. It wouldn't be long before the rocks began to pile up, closing the narrow tunnel behind them.

"Look out!" Liam shouted suddenly.

Rory shrank against the tunnel wall, turning away and covering her head with her arms. A shower of smaller rock beat at her neck and shoulders. When the rattling rain of stone ceased, she started toward Liam.

"Are you hurt?" he asked.

"No." She pressed her lips together, fighting her fear. Liam rolled another rock toward her, and she pushed it down the tunnel, shoving it into the darkness.

The rats were thinning out, she realized, on her way back. Either there were fewer coming out of the mine, or the rocks were scaring them off.

Liam worked in silence. Rory moved the rocks as fast as she could, duck-walking in the narrow tunnel, sagging against the side to catch her breath whenever she could. After a long time, she cleared her throat, tasting coal dust. "Can you tell anything? Are we going to be able to make it through?"

Liam didn't answer. Rory was afraid to ask again.

Liam wanted to give up. His arms were aching. Every muscle in his body was cramped, and his knees were bruised and cut. His hands were worst of all. They were sticky with blood again, and every time he dragged another rock free, the pain was almost more than he could stand.

He couldn't answer Rory's questions. What did she expect him to say? He had no way to know how deep the rockfall was. He passed Rory another chunk of flattened stone. His thoughts kept churning. If he had just been a few minutes earlier to work, he would have been with his Da. But that would have left Rory alone through all this. He wondered if Nolan was still alive. Maybe not. The air had been going fast.

Liam loosened another rock. The flow of air was increasing. He could feel rats running past him.

"Liam?"

She sounded desperate. He half-turned. "Yes?"

"Can't you tell *anything*?"

He started to answer this time, reaching out with his right hand to steady himself as he leaned back to rest for a moment. His fingers touched a flat surface and he found himself turning toward it, tracing the width of an enormous rock—one that was so big, it very nearly filled the width of the tunnel. His fingers flew over the big stone. He would never be able to lift it, much less move it.

He sat down heavily, and a rat ran across his legs. He could hear the rats scratching their way upward and he hated them for being so small, for making it out so easily.

"Liam?"

He drew in a long breath, intending to tell her about the big rock, but not to worry, that they could sit right here, breathing the fresher air until someone found them. But before he could open his mouth there was a sound of trickling sand and clattering pebbles from above, then a loud rumble of falling stone.

"Get clear!" Liam lurched, stumbling into Rory. For a moment they struggled to free themselves from each other, then, with her leading, they crawled as fast as they could. After a minute or so, Liam stopped, breathing hard. The fall was over.

"Rory? You all right?"

She made a small, frightened sound, but he could hear her coming toward him. He made his way back up the tunnel with her following at his heels. He sat down, hoping that the rock-fall hadn't frightened her too much. This was still the safest place. He drew in a long, dusty breath and coughed.

Trying not to panic, he turned slowly, facing the rock that blocked the tunnel. The air had gone dead, still. The cool flow that had cleared his thinking and raised his hopes was gone. The last rockfall had cut off the air.

"Liam? Are you hurt?"

"No," he said slowly, wondering if he should tell her.

"Do you want me to dig for a while? Are you tired?"

Liam could hear the worry in Rory's voice and he knew he should say something. But what? They couldn't go back down. The air had been bad—really bad.

"Liam?"

"We can't get out this way," he said sadly.

He heard her cough. Then she cleared her throat. "What do you mean? Did the falling rock—"

"There's a boulder jammed across the passage. It's too big to move. The rockfall was on the far side of it. Rory, the air passage is gone." Liam could hear her ragged breathing and he wanted to reach out and hold her hand, but he was afraid that if he moved at all, she would start to scream again.

"What should we do?" she asked, finally. Her voice was tight, controlled.

"We have to stay here," Liam told her. "The air is still better than it was down below."

"If there's an explosion from the dust, we're safer here, aren't we?" she asked, and he knew she was thinking about her father and brother.

"Yes," he told her, not at all sure that it was true.

"But, Liam . . ."

He heard her shifting around, and there was a wildness coming back into her voice. He covered his face with his hands and slumped against the wall of the tunnel.

"What are we going to do, Liam?" Her voice was shrill. "Just tell me—"

"Tell you what?" he cut her off, desperate to stop the high-pitched hammering of her voice. "I couldn't help my father or Nolan and I never should have let you come down into the mine at all and—"

"Liam!"

He stopped, startled by her sudden calm

intensity. He felt her hand on his arm. "I'm sorry, Liam. You've done everything you could do."

He swallowed hard, tears stinging his eyes. "I don't know if that's true, Rory." He took in a long breath. "I'm scared."

"I am, too," she whispered.

He covered her hand with his, and they sat together in silence. Liam said prayers for a long time, then thought about his mother. He knew Rory was thinking the same kinds of things, and it made him even sadder.

The sound of picks striking rock startled them both. Liam looked up, then began to shout. A second later, Rory joined in, and he could hear men yelling from above. Rory led the way back down the tunnel and they wait-ed, cowering when rock bounced toward them in the dark. Liam gave her his cap and he could hear her struggling to make sure all of her hair was beneath it.

Liam stood aside as the miners pulled Rory up into the gangway of the Seven-Foot Vein. The twinkling of their lamps was the most beautiful sight in the world to him. Rory was crying softly.

"There's a driver and his mule hurt down there," Liam said hoarsely as the men brought him out. "And my Da is on the other side of a fall a mile further in—"

"Help has already gone in from the slope side, son," one of the miners interrupted him. "That's the way you'll go out. The shaft is blocked."

Liam nodded, hoping Da was safe by now. "Nolan wouldn't leave his mule—" he began.

"Tell us where," one of the miners interrupted him.

Liam explained where Nolan was. The moment he finished speaking, three of the miners started down the connector tunnel.

"We could hear the cave-ins and we saw the rats streaming out," someone said from behind Liam. He turned and saw a tall, thin boy not much older than himself. "I thought I heard screaming. So Papa figured we'd best dig a ways and see."

"Thank you," Liam said, and the boy grinned. Rory was standing off by herself, silent, the cap pulled low over her eyes.

"You'll walk them out to the slope lift, Terrence?" one of the men asked. The boy nodded and pointed down the gangway. Liam led off, gesturing for Rory to stay close.

As they walked, Terrence kept asking questions. Liam answered once or twice. Rory was quiet. The sound of the lift engines grew steadily louder, but Liam found his joy and relief fading into a dull exhaustion. His hands were in bad shape, and his knees weren't any better. The rest of him felt like he had been in a losing fight. Rory was walking slowly, her head down. He could tell she didn't feel any better than he did. When Terrence left them, they both mumbled a thanks and farewell.

Back out in the sunshine, Liam blinked and squinted. His eyes streamed as he watched the line of rescue workers filing toward the slope. There were two men lying on stretchers—one of them with a bloody pant leg—but Da was nowhere to be seen.

Liam turned back to Rory. She was grimacing, her eyes half closed against the painful light. Her face was blackened, and there were streaks in the coal dust from where she had cried. Stumbling and shaky in the glaring sunshine, they set off toward the shaft, Rory keeping the cap low on her forehead.

They skirted St. John's patch with its rows of identical houses, then stayed on the far side of the creek, passing the cemetery. Liam saw Rory glancing at the headstones. As they got closer to the breaker building, he wondered if she would just head home, but she stayed with him, shrugging Paddy's jacket higher, turning the collar up to hide her face.

Liam led the way through the milling crowd around the breaker, searching the faces as he went. Men were talking in low, terse voices. Some of them still had clean faces—they hadn't been underground yet today. Liam glanced toward the breaker door. A steady stream of clean-faced miners were going inside carrying picks and shovels.

"There," Rory whispered urgently, tugging at his sleeve. "Your Da. There he is."

Liam turned, afraid to believe her. But Da was coming toward him, arms held wide. They hugged, and Liam felt his feet leave the ground as his father swung him in a slow circle, then set him down. When Liam stepped away, he saw his father glance at Rory. She had tucked her chin against her chest. Only the blackened side of her cheek showed.

"I was on my way to help dig," Da was saying. Then he noticed Liam's hands. "Jesus, Mary, and Joseph," he swore softly. "You go on home and let Mrs. Hamilton see to those."

"I'll come with you," Liam said.

Da shook his head. "You go on home, and get the lad back to his family, too." He looked at Rory. "If there's danger-pay for this day, I'll see to it you get your share."

Liam watched Rory nod, a small, jerky motion that didn't reveal her face.

"You two go on," Da said. He hugged Liam again, a short, fierce hug this time, then turned and picked up a shovel from a line of tools leaning against the wall. He disappeared through the breaker door.

"Can you get home all right?" Liam asked, drawing Rory to one side.

He saw a glint of mischief in her eye, then she ducked her head again. "It'll be the easiest part of the whole day, Liam. The hard part will be trying to explain all this to Mama."

"I'm sorry," Liam began, but she put out her hand.

"It was my idea."

He shook her hand gently, solemnly, seeing for the first time that her palms were nearly as raw as his own.

"See you at supper, Liam," she said quietly. "I'll pray for Nolan."

He nodded. He wanted to talk to her, to talk about everything that had happened, but that would have to come later. He waved at her, smiling, then he headed for the shaft, picking up a shovel as his father had done.